BABE RUTH

Name: George Herman "Babe" Ruth, Jr.
Born: February 6, 1895
Died: August 16, 1948
Position: Baseball Player—Pitcher and Slugger

Career Highlights:

- Broke baseball's most important hitting records, including most years leading a league in home runs, and highest slugging percentage for a season.
- His home run record (714) stood until 1974.
- One of the first five players inducted into the Baseball Hall of Fame.

Interesting Facts:

- Was first introduced to baseball by the monks who ran the orphanage and reformatory where Babe was sent at the age of seven.
- Even today, the old Yankee Stadium is known as the "house that Ruth built."

BABE RUTH

HISTORY'S ★ ★ALL-STARS
BABE RUTH

By **Guernsey Van Riper Jr.**
Illustrated by **Seymour Fleishman**

ALADDIN
New York   London   Toronto   Sydney   New Delhi

ALADDIN

An imprint of Simon & Schuster Children's Publishing Division
1230 Avenue of the Americas, New York, NY 10020
First Aladdin edition February 2015
Copyright © 1954, 1959 by Bobbs-Merrill Company Inc.
Cover illustration © 2015 by Chris Whetzel
All rights reserved, including the right of reproduction in whole or in part in any form.
ALADDIN is a trademark of Simon & Schuster, Inc., and related logo is a registered trademark of Simon & Schuster, Inc.
For information about special discounts for bulk purchases, please contact Simon & Schuster Special Sales at 1-866-506-1949 or business@simonandschuster.com.
Cover designed by Laura Lyn DiSiena
Designed by Mike Rosamilia
The text of this book was set in Caslon Pro.
Manufactured in the United States of America 0115 OFF
2 4 6 8 10 9 7 5 3 1
Library of Congress Control Number 2014933330
ISBN 978-1-4814-2509-4 (hc)
ISBN 978-1-4814-2507-0 (pbk)
ISBN 978-1-4814-3079-1 (eBook)
Originally published as Childhood of Famous Americans.

*To the Brothers of the Xaverian Order
this book is respectfully dedicated*

The Babe Ruth Story, by Babe Ruth as told to Bob Considine, published by E. P. Dutton & Co., was a particularly valuable reference book in the preparation of this volume. The author is also especially indebted to Brother Herman, Brother Xaverius, Brother Benjamin, and Brother Hilaire for many courtesies in supplying material on which this story is based. Among the many other books which have assisted him, *Babe Ruth*, by Martin Weldon, published by Thomas Y. Crowell Co., has been unusually helpful to the author.

★ ILLUSTRATIONS ★

Numerous smaller illustrations

★ CONTENTS ★

OH, THAT GEORGE!

THE DOOR OF the little restaurant flew open. A tall, seven-year-old boy dashed out. *Bang!* went the door as it closed behind him. Headlong he ran along West Camden Street in Baltimore. It was a warm day in April 1902.

The boy nearly collided with two women walking toward him.

"Georgie! Georgie Ruth!" called the shorter woman sharply. "Watch where you're going!"

George stopped suddenly. He thrust back the mop of dark-brown hair from his forehead. He grinned sheepishly. "'Scuse me, Mrs. Callahan," he said. "I'm in a hurry!" He pushed past the women on the narrow sidewalk and ran down the street as fast as he could go.

Both women turned to watch.

"That boy!" said Mrs. Callahan. She shook her head. "But I guess it isn't his fault. He hardly has anyone to look after him."

"Why, what's the matter?" asked her companion, with a concerned look.

"Well, his father and mother work awfully hard trying to make a living in that little restaurant. Half the time Mrs. Ruth is sick. And she's got a daughter, Mamie, to look after. So nobody pays much attention to George."

"Oh, that's too bad!"

Mrs. Callahan sighed. "And the things that go on in that restaurant! The men seem to do nothing but fight and talk loudly."

"Are they sailors and oystermen?" her companion asked.

"Yes, and the roughest kind, I'm afraid. It's certainly the wrong place for a headstrong boy like that George Ruth. One of these days I've a mind to call the police."

ON THE STREET

George whirled around the next corner. He was bubbling with energy. He caught up with three boys walking along halfway down the block.

"Hiya, Slats!" he shouted to a thin-faced, sandy-haired boy. George slapped him on the back in greeting.

Slats stumbled and nearly fell. He gulped hard before he could speak. "Hey, what's the idea?" he managed to say. He picked up a stick and started for George.

George burst out laughing. "What's the matter?" he roared. "Can't you take a joke?"

The other two boys laughed too.

"I thought you were tough, Slats," shouted one, a short red-haired boy.

"I guess George doesn't know how strong he is," said the boy named Jim.

"Well, lay off me," growled Slats, still waving his stick.

The boys walked along the sidewalk.

"Where are we going now?" asked Red.

"Down to the docks!" George shouted. "Come on!"

"Hey, wait a minute," Jim said. "Isn't anyone going to school?"

"Ha, ha, ha!" laughed the other three boys.

"What'd you bring Jim along for, Red?" asked Slats.

"Why, what's the matter?" Jim asked.

"I never have been to school," George boasted in a loud voice.

"Why, what about your mom and pop?" Jim asked in surprise. "Don't they care?"

"Aw, they're too busy to know what I do," George answered. "They wanted me to go, but I wouldn't."

He was bragging very loudly. It made him feel big. But he suddenly remembered how sad Mom had been when he refused to go. He didn't feel quite so sure of himself.

"Aren't you ever going?" asked Jim, still surprised.

"Well, maybe someday," George said.

"What for?" Slats jeered. "I only go when I have to."

"Oh—I—" George stammered. He couldn't stop thinking about Mom lying upstairs in bed, about her begging him to go to school and to

stay out of trouble. It made him feel so bad that he couldn't answer Slats.

But George didn't like to feel bad. He looked around for something to do—quickly.

"Hey, look!" he shouted. There on the sidewalk was a trash can filled with old rubbish. He gave the can a big shove. It upset in the gutter. Cans and bottles and old rags flew all over the street.

"Let's go!" shouted George. All the boys ran as hard as they could. But Slats suddenly tripped George with his stick. Down he went, sprawling full length on the sidewalk! Slats roared with laughter as he and the other boys raced around the corner.

A woman carrying a broom hurried out of a nearby house. "You young ruffians!" she shouted. She rushed toward George with her broom. But George jumped to his feet and raced after the boys.

"I'll get you, Slats!" he shouted. He was so angry he couldn't think of anything else. He caught up with the boys at the next corner. But Slats kept dancing away from him, waving his stick back and forth.

"We're even! We're even!" called Slats. He grinned in a sly way. But George was still angry. He kept charging at Slats.

"Hey, George, I know where we can get some oysters!" Slats shouted.

George stopped chasing Slats. If there was anything George liked, it was oysters. And he was always hungry. Even if the Ruths had a restaurant, George never seemed to get enough to eat.

"No fooling?" he asked Slats doubtfully.

"No fooling!" said Slats. "All we can eat, and they're just waiting for us. Come on!"

George grinned broadly. "You bet I will!"

he shouted. "Lead me to them!"

George and Slats and Red ran off toward the docks, chattering gaily. They didn't ask Jim to go with them. They knew he wouldn't.

Jim watched them a minute. Then he shook his head and started for school.

TROUBLE IN THE RESTAURANT

It was six o'clock in the evening when George got home. He looked cautiously through the door of the restaurant before going in. Only Pop was working behind the counter. "Mom must still be sick," George thought.

About half the tables in the place were full. All the customers were rough-looking men who worked around the Baltimore docks. They were shouting at Mr. Ruth to hurry up with their orders.

George pushed open the door. He waved to

Pop and hurried toward the stairs at the back of the dining room.

Suddenly a huge, bearded man jumped up. "There's one of those kids now!" he shouted, pointing at George. "There were three of them, grabbing oysters when we were unloading!"

He reached out to get George as he went by. George dodged quickly. He made a face at the big man and dashed for the stairs. But he moved so quickly he bumped against one of the tables. Dishes and glasses slid off the table and crashed to the floor. A sailor sitting at the table jumped up.

"Now look what you did!" he shouted at the bearded man. "What's the idea going after that kid? Pick on someone your own size!"

The big oysterman turned to the sailor. "You look about my size," he roared. He rushed at the sailor, swinging both fists.

Other men jumped up to take sides. In an instant almost everyone had pitched in. Tables and chairs were overturned, dishes crashed on the floor. The men shouted and wrestled and hit anyone they could.

"Here, stop that!" shouted Mr. Ruth. "Let's

have some order!" He tried to stop the fighting. He was a big man, but he was pushed aside easily by the struggling crowd.

George stood on the stairs, watching. "My gosh," he thought, "I didn't mean to start anything like this! They're breaking up the restaurant! Why did that oysterman have to be here?"

Then he got interested in the fight. He shouted encouragement to the sailor who was fighting the oysterman. George had joined in many a rough battle with other boys on the docks and around the streets. He had seen many fights among the sailors and dockworkers. He didn't think about people getting hurt. He forgot about everything being broken in the restaurant. He shouted and swung his fists just as though he were in the midst of it.

Suddenly the door flew open. Shrill whistles sounded. Two burly policemen rushed in. "All right, all right, break it up!" they shouted.

"I don't want the cops to get me," thought George. He hurried up the stairs.

Mom was propped up in bed. Her thin, pale face looked worried and frightened. George's sister, Mamie, was sitting beside the bed. She looked frightened, too.

"George! What's happening?" his mother asked.

"Oh, it was a wonderful fight!" George said. "Pop tried to stop it, but there were too many men. They just pushed him aside. Gee, it was something! Men were sprawled on the floor. Then two big cops had to come in and take over. They're stopping the fight now."

"George! Everything in the restaurant will be ruined! How can you talk that way? We've had a hard enough time without this!"

George's heart sank. He suddenly remembered that he was the cause of the fight. And he knew how hard his parents worked. How would they ever buy new tables and chairs and dishes?

"How can you like those terrible fights?" asked Mamie.

George frowned. "Oh, you're a girl. What do you know about fights?" But he worried more and more. He knew he was really to blame for the trouble.

Down below, the restaurant got quieter. The door banged as the men left. Soon there were footsteps on the stairs. Pop walked in—and right behind him one of the policemen!

"Sorry to bother you, ma'am," said the officer. "But I was telling your husband here that you'll have to keep the place more orderly. Especially with these children around."

"Why, we do the best we can in this neighborhood," Mrs. Ruth said sadly.

"That's what I was saying," Mr. Ruth agreed.

The policeman went on: "And, I'm sorry to say, I've been hearing bad reports about your boy. He's going to be in serious trouble if he's not careful."

Everybody looked at George. At first he was so angry he started to shout back at the officer. Then he thought, "Mom and Pop will just get the blame if I do. I didn't mean to make all this trouble." He hung his head and said nothing.

"We'll do the best we can," Mrs. Ruth said.

A FRIENDLY SUGGESTION

The next day George stayed home. He helped Pop clean up the restaurant. He was still feeling very bad about the fight. He looked at all the broken dishes and tables and chairs. How could all this have happened? Just because he and the kids had picked up a few oysters.

He wondered what Slats and Red were doing.

If he could only be out running around with them instead of being cooped up in the restaurant! Then he thought sadly that he probably would do something else wrong. Maybe the police would be watching for him. "Maybe I'm just no good," he said to himself.

"George, you pile those broken things outside," Pop said. "I'm going upstairs to talk to your mother."

"All right, Pop," said George.

Mr. Ruth looked around as he started for the stairs. He shook his head. The place looked terrible.

"How are you feeling, Kate?" he asked as he walked into Mrs. Ruth's room.

"A little better," Mrs. Ruth said. "Maybe I can be up again in a day or two. But tell me, dear, how is the restaurant?"

Mr. Ruth shook his head. "It's pretty bad. I

don't know if we can open up tonight or not. We'll have to get new tables and chairs and dishes. And how are we going to do that?" He thought a minute. Then he said, "But if we don't open up, how can we make a living?"

"I just don't know," Mrs. Ruth said. "And Mamie and George both need new clothes."

Mr. Ruth sighed. "What are we going to do about that boy? We've shut our eyes for too long. He's always in trouble."

"Now you know it isn't all his fault," Mrs. Ruth replied. "We have to take some of the blame, even though we didn't realize he was running so wild. I've been sick, and we've both been so busy we haven't been able to look after him properly. Maybe that's how he got so head-strong."

"He needs a good licking," Mr. Ruth said. "Besides, if he were in school where he belongs, he wouldn't have time for so much trouble. He should have started this term, as soon as he got over his sprained ankle. Maybe they'll still take him for the rest of the term."

Mrs. Ruth sighed. "Surely he'll agree to go now, after all the trouble last night."

They heard footsteps on the stairs.

"Is that George?" asked Mrs. Ruth.

Pop went to the door. "Oh, it's Mrs. Callahan from next door. Will you come in?"

"Thank you," Mrs. Callahan said. "I do hope you're feeling better, Mrs. Ruth. I'm sorry to hear about all the disturbance last night."

"Yes," said Mrs. Ruth, "the fighting is very bad for the children."

Mrs. Callahan said, "I hope you won't mind, but that's just what I came to talk about."

"Why, what do you mean?" Pop asked.

"Please don't be angry," Mrs. Callahan said

with a smile. "I don't want you to think I'm just a nosy neighbor. But I know you've been worried about George—and I have a suggestion."

"We'd be glad to hear it," said Mrs. Ruth, motioning to Pop to listen quietly.

"Well," Mrs. Callahan said, "there's a very good school right here in Baltimore that might help George a lot. It's the St. Mary's Industrial School for Boys, over at Caton and Wilkins Avenues. It's run by the Brothers of the Xaverian Order. They're Catholic brothers who do good work for boys in many different countries."

"H'mph," Mr. Ruth growled. "How would that help George?"

"You see," said Mrs. Callahan, "the brothers could become his guardians until he's twenty-one. He could live at the school. He could do his regular schoolwork, and he would learn a trade, too."

After Mrs. Callahan left, Mr. and Mrs. Ruth talked it all over. Finally Mrs. Ruth said, "I just hate to think of George's going away from home. Of course it might be for his own good. We have to think of that. I—I know they'd take good care of him, and that would make it easier for us to look after Mamie. But I just don't know what to say."

"I hate to think we can't look after our own children," Pop said angrily. He thought a minute. "If George will agree to go to a public school, maybe we can make out somehow. Let's talk to him."

When George came into the room he was sure he was going to be scolded. He hung his head and shuffled his feet. "I didn't mean to make all that trouble," he said. "I—I'll be more careful next time. If I only had lots of money I'd buy you a new restaurant."

Worried as she was, this made his mother smile. "I'm sure you would, Georgie," she said. "But there's an easier way. All you have to do is to start school right now and promise to stay away from the docks. That'll make both of us very happy."

George looked up quickly. Start school? He couldn't do that! He'd be so far behind the others that they'd all laugh at him. Besides, Red and Slats would make fun of him after the way

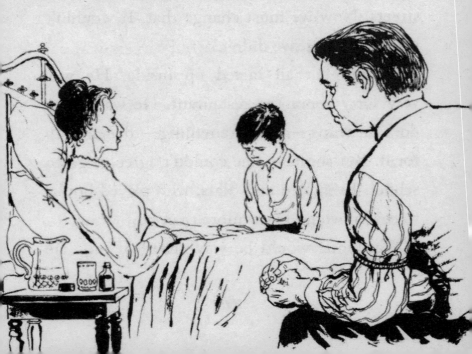

he had boasted. And to be cooped up in school all day—and to stay away from the docks? He just couldn't!

"Why, what's the matter, Georgie?" asked his father. "You can surely do that, after all the trouble you've caused."

"Please listen to me, Georgie," said Mom. "You're not a bad boy. You're kind and generous and friendly, but I'm afraid we've let you get a bad start in life. We've just let you run in the streets. Now we must change that. It wouldn't be fair to you if we didn't."

George felt all mixed up inside. He was very sorry about the restaurant. He wanted to do something—almost anything—to make up for it. But somehow he couldn't agree to go to school. Even Red and Slats, who played hooky so much, would know more than he.

"Everyone would be way ahead of me," he

mumbled, "and Red and Slats would call me a baby."

"Oh, Georgie, you'd catch up! And you'll have to stay away from those two boys anyway. You just don't think straight when you're with them," his mother said. "They're headed for trouble, the same as you are if you don't listen to your father and me!"

Still George couldn't say yes. He wanted to do what Mom and Pop said, but he just couldn't. He didn't want to be behind everyone else. He shook his head. He felt miserable.

"I—I can't promise," he said.

Mrs. Ruth wiped the tears from her eyes. She spoke to Mr. Ruth softly. "You'd better tell him about St. Mary's School. I—I'm afraid he needs it even more than we thought."

AT ST. MARY'S

GEORGE GULPED. He stood in the bare
office looking at the man at the desk. He felt
like rushing to the door and calling out, "Pop!
Come and get me!" For his father had just left
him at the St. Mary's School.

The man in the long black robe stood up
behind the desk. "Come on over here and sit
down, George," he said in a kindly voice.

George shifted his feet. He looked at the black
robe. "I—I feel as if I'm in jail," he thought. He
didn't move.

But the man didn't notice. He went on speaking. "I am Brother Dominic, and I hope you're going to like it here. It would be my fault if you didn't like it, because I am in charge."

George was surprised. Brother Dominic didn't talk like a jailer! George looked at him more closely. There was a smile on his square, kindly face. He beckoned to George. Without thinking, George sat down in the chair by the desk. Still the young boy felt very strange. He had never been in any place like this before.

"Don't worry, lad, we'll take care of you," Brother Dominic said. He opened a drawer and pulled out a paper sack. "Here, maybe you'd like some of these." He handed George several sugar cookies.

George's mouth hung open in astonishment. Was this the way they treated you when you wouldn't go to school? He reached for the cookies. He tried one. It was so good that he ate all he had in a hurry.

Brother Dominic chuckled merrily. He noticed that George was smiling for the first time. He handed the boy the bag of cookies.

George's grin got bigger and bigger. He took the bag and finished off the last three cookies.

"I'm sorry we couldn't take you in April," said Brother Dominic, "but we're pretty crowded here. Let's see now." He took up a paper. "George Herman Ruth, born on February 6, 1895—and this is June 13, 1902." He looked up. "That makes you about seven and a half years old. You're pretty tall for your age, aren't you?" Brother Dominic paused for a moment, then he said, "Since you haven't been in school before, George, the right place for you to start out is in first grade."

George frowned. This was what he had been

dreading. "You mean, I have to start with the little kids?"

Brother Dominic chuckled. "Well, there are some little fellows, and there are some fellows even bigger than you. I don't think you'll feel out of place."

But George wasn't convinced. "They'll all be ahead of me," he protested. "They'll all know more than I do."

"Is that bad?" asked Brother Dominic. "You have to start sometime."

"I guess," George said unhappily. "But I don't want anyone to be ahead of me."

Brother Dominic rubbed his jaw in silence. Then he said, "Well, George, I'm glad to know that you want to do well in school. It's a good thing to want to be first. But I'll be satisfied if you just do your best."

Hearing a noise, George looked out the

window. In the big play yard behind the gray stone buildings he saw a huge crowd of boys running and shouting. There were hundreds of them. And he didn't know one of them! How would he ever get to know all these strange boys? They all belonged here! And they would probably all make fun of him because he had just arrived.

George frowned. He felt very lonely as he turned back to Brother Dominic. Maybe Brother Dominic was friendly, but how about the boys?

George suddenly felt frightened. "What am I doing here, anyway?" he thought. "I'll have to do what they say all the time. I can't run around in the streets. I'll have to go to school, and the other boys will all know more than I do."

George jumped from his chair. "I—I don't want to stay here!" he blurted out. "I want to go back to Mom and Pop!"

Brother Dominic smiled. "George," he said, "I know just what will make you feel at home. You come along with me." He took George's hand and started out the door.

"No!" shouted George, pulling back. "I want to go home!"

"Now, George, you've got to give me a chance. You'll change your mind—just wait and see."

Out they went into the big yard.

George kept tugging at Brother Dominic's hand, trying to get free.

"I'll show you a good way to work off that energy," said Brother Dominic. "Look!"

There were three baseball diamonds on the huge playground. The boys brought bats and balls and gloves. They spread out over the diamonds, tossing the balls back and forth.

"What's that?" George asked. He had never seen a game of baseball before.

Brother Dominic was startled. "Why, son, you've got a treat ahead of you! Baseball is our national game."

They walked up to a diamond where boys about George's age were playing. A game was starting. George thought how silly the batter looked—waggling his bat, trying to hit the ball.

Another black-robed man walked over to Brother Dominic and George.

Brother Dominic greeted him. "Brother Herman, I have a new recruit for you. Here's George Ruth, who has never seen a game of baseball."

"Hello, George," said Brother Herman. "So you've never seen a baseball game before! We'll fix that! I'll get you in the game pretty soon. How would you like that?"

He spoke eagerly, his dark eyes flashing. George couldn't help liking him.

"Well—" George hesitated. They were just trying to get him to stay. He wouldn't do it! "Aw, who wants to throw an old ball?" he mumbled glumly.

Just then the catcher reached for a wide pitch with his bare hand. He couldn't quite catch it. The ball struck him on the finger. "Ouch!" he yelled. But he picked up the ball and threw it back to the pitcher. Then he rubbed his sore finger very gently.

Brother Herman hurried over. He inspected the boy's hand. "Looks like a sprain, Joe," he said. "You'd better run up to the infirmary."

Joe didn't want to go, but Brother Herman sent him on his way. Brother Herman took the catcher's mitt and walked over to George. "Here's where you learn baseball, young fellow," he said. "You're the new catcher for the Brownies."

"Me?" said George. In spite of himself, he was curious about the mitt Brother Herman held out to him. But he hesitated. He could feel all the boys looking at him.

When he didn't move they all shouted, "Come on! Play ball!"

Before he knew what was happening, Brother Herman put the mitt on George's hand and walked him up to home plate.

"All right, Johnny, throw him a few!" Brother Herman called to the pitcher.

The batter stepped aside. Johnny wound up and threw the ball straight at George.

"Hey!" shouted George, standing awkwardly behind the plate.

Without thinking he stuck up his glove to protect himself. *Plunk!* The ball landed right in the mitt.

Brother Herman grinned at Brother Dominic.

All the boys shouted and whistled. George looked at the ball, surprised. Maybe this wasn't so bad after all!

"Let's have it back!" Johnny shouted.

George looked at the ball. How could he throw it back? It was lying in the mitt on his left hand. And he always threw things with his left hand. Suddenly he grabbed off the mitt with his right hand, seized the ball with his left and

pegged it back to Johnny. It was a good throw, right to the pitcher.

"That's the way!" Johnny shouted. He wound up and threw again.

This time George put the mitt on his right hand. It didn't fit right, but still he caught the ball. It felt good when the ball plunked into the mitt. Eagerly he grabbed the ball and returned it to the pitcher. He put the mitt back on his left hand.

"Come on, batter up!" the boys shouted. The batter stepped to the plate. George put on the odd-looking catcher's mask. The game went on. Half the time George didn't know just what to do. But he went after every ball. He caught most of them. He still had to yank off the glove every time he wanted to throw. But his throws to the pitcher were straight and true.

He forgot about Brother Dominic and

Brother Herman. He forgot about where he was. He forgot to feel angry. All he could think of was catching the ball and throwing it back. He could do anything these other kids could do!

"Strike three!" Brother Herman called. The last batter was out in the first half of the first inning.

The Brownies all threw down their gloves. They rushed to sit down on a hard bench. The Greenies ran onto the field.

George stood wondering what to do.

A chunky boy seized the mitt off his hand. "Go on, stupid," he shouted, shoving George out of the catcher's position.

George's temper flared up. "Don't call me stupid!" he shouted. He drew back his fist.

Brother Herman stepped between them. "That will do, Rod," he said to the chunky boy. "That was nice catching, George," he went on. "Come on over to the bench and meet the other Brownies."

He guided the angry George away.

"Boys, meet your new catcher—George Ruth," he said. "George, here are the rest of the boys on the team." He rattled off their names so fast that George couldn't remember even one! Finally Brother Herman said, "And I guess you know Johnny Peters, your pitcher."

Then Brother Herman went to the plate to umpire. George sat down on the bench beside Johnny, a sandy-haired, freckle-faced boy.

"You're the first left-handed catcher I've seen," Johnny said. "Did you ever do much catching before? Why, you're better than Joe!"

"Joe?" George tried to remember which one he was.

"The boy who got hurt."

"Oh! Why, I never even played baseball before."

"You're kidding!"

"Don't you believe me?" shouted George, jumping up. He was still feeling strange with all these new boys. And his temper easily got the best of him.

Johnny just laughed. "Sure I believe you," he said. "But you're pretty good just to be starting. Want me to tell you about the game?"

George felt a little silly for getting angry. He grinned at Johnny. He wanted very much to know all about baseball. And Johnny didn't act like the kind of boy who would make fun of him for not knowing anything about the sport. "Sure!" George said. "It's a pretty good game."

He sat down and watched the Brownies take their turn at bat. Johnny explained the game to him. George began to get the hang of it. Soon he was shouting as loudly as the others, "Come on, get a hit!"

Finally, in the third inning, George got his turn to bat. Neither team had scored. George grabbed a bat and walked to the plate. He decided he was going to hit the ball a mile. But when he got there he felt awkward. How did you go about hitting the ball, anyway? He swung the bat a couple of times. Then the Greenie pitcher wound up and threw the ball right over the plate. George just watched it go by.

"Strike one!" Brother Herman called.

George gripped the bat tighter. This wasn't so easy after all.

The pitcher threw again. George swung with all his might. He swung so hard he turned all the way around, lost his balance, and sat down on the ground.

"You missed it by a mile!" shouted the chunky Greenie catcher.

Everyone shouted and laughed as George got

up. George scowled at the catcher, but he didn't say anything. He hated to have the boys laugh at him.

He heard Johnny shout, "That's the way to go after it, George! You'll hit it next time." He felt a little better. He got set at the plate. "I'll show 'em," he thought.

Here came the ball! George swung as hard as he could. He hit the ball high and far down the right-field line. He stood and watched it.

"Foul ball," Brother Herman called.

Maybe it was only a foul ball, but George couldn't forget the thrill he felt when the bat connected solidly with the ball. Why, this was the most fun he'd ever had!

George got set again. The pitcher threw, and George swung with all his might. He missed completely!

"Wow!" said Johnny, as he started for the

pitcher's mound. "If you ever hit one, it'll be a home run for sure."

"I'll hit one. Just you wait!"

But George didn't get another chance that day. The game lasted only five innings. The Brownies lost, 2–0.

George was eager to go right on playing. But a loud bell rang out from the bell tower on the main school building. The other boys scattered, carrying their gloves and balls and bats.

"Time for supper," Johnny shouted. "Come on, George!"

George didn't need a second invitation. He was *always* hungry!

BIG BROTHER MATTHIAS

"HERE WE ARE! Dormitory Six! Here's where you will sleep." Brother Herman took George into the big room on the fourth floor of the main school building.

Supper was over, and George was feeling pretty good. He had sat with Johnny in the huge dining room. He had had plenty to eat. In fact, Johnny had teased him about how much he had put away!

"Here's your bed," said Brother Herman, indicating one of the white iron beds near the center of the room.

George looked around. There were seventy beds in neat rows, but to George they looked like a thousand.

Just then, boys poured through the door into the dormitory. Laughing and talking, they scattered through the room.

George caught sight of Johnny, way up in a corner of the room. But he didn't know any of the boys around him. Again he felt strange.

"Here's your nightshirt," Brother Herman said. "You must be undressed by seven-thirty. Lights go out at eight. Just let me know if you need anything."

George sat down on the wooden chair beside his bed. Brother Herman walked around the room talking to the boys. Nobody paid any attention to George. He wished he could talk to someone. A couple of rows over he caught sight of Rod, the catcher on the Greenie team. "Aw, he doesn't like me," George said to himself. Still, though, he thought he might call to Rod.

Then he saw Rod point to him. Rod said something to another boy. Then they both laughed. George flushed in embarrassment and anger. He doubled up his fists. He felt like rushing over and taking a swing at Rod.

"If I were only at home, I could go out on the street and meet some of the kids," George thought. "Instead I have to sit here in this old room and let that Rod make fun of me!"

"All right, boys, get undressed," called Brother Herman, who was standing at the door.

Still angry, George undressed. He watched the other boys put their clothes neatly on their chairs. In a few minutes they all knelt to say their prayers. They climbed into bed, and at eight o'clock the lights went out.

George didn't feel sleepy. So many things

had happened today! He had enjoyed playing baseball, and Johnny had been friendly. But none of the other boys seemed to like him. The Brothers were very kind, but now he'd have to do everything they said.

He had never slept away from home before. If he were at home, Mom would come in to see that he was in bed. All of a sudden he thought, "Why, it'll be this way every night! When will I see Mom and Pop again?"

His eyes smarted, and he rubbed them angrily. It was all he could do to keep from bursting into tears. "Only babies cry," he thought. Still he couldn't get over feeling sad. The more he thought about it, the sadder he got. "I can't stay here!" he decided.

He peered around the dark room. Everything was quiet. No one stirred in the rows of white beds. George crept out of bed. He put on his stockings. He pulled on his pants. He carefully gathered up the rest of his clothes. On his tiptoes he crept out of the room.

Down the long flight of stairs he went, walking quietly. Finally he reached the main floor—and he hadn't seen a soul!

He breathed a great sigh. Carefully he turned the knob of the front door. It was locked! He tiptoed over to a window. Very quietly he climbed onto a chair to unlock it. Then he tugged as hard as he could. Up went the window without making a sound.

But then George stopped. The outside of the window was covered with heavy wire netting. He couldn't get out! Desperately George seized the netting and shook it with all his might. He could hardly move it, but he did make a lot of noise. He stopped and looked around. Had anyone heard? Would he be in trouble if someone found him here?

There was a footfall down the corridor behind him. George turned in alarm. Then he thought his heart would stop beating. Looming up in front of him was—a—a giant!

"What's the trouble, son? Can I help you?" came a soft, pleasant voice.

The light went on. Now George saw a very tall, powerful-looking man, dressed in a long black robe. No wonder he had looked like a giant in the dark. George had never seen such a big man before. But he had a pleasant face, with blue eyes and very light hair.

George gulped. "I want to go home," he said at last.

"Why, you're George Ruth! I'm glad to meet you. I'm Brother Matthias. Now, aren't you going to stay with us even one night?"

"I'm locked in!" George said.

"Well, come on and sit down, and we'll

find out what's the trouble." Brother Matthias motioned to a chair. "You know, Brother Dominic will be very unhappy if he hears you want to leave already. I don't think you'd want to hurt his feelings, now would you?"

George had forgotten about Brother Dominic. Yes, Brother Dominic had been nice. He had given him the cookies and had taken him to the baseball game. "Of course I don't want to hurt his feelings," George thought. "Only—"

"And you know your parents are going to feel very bad if you go home now. They didn't want you to leave in the first place. But they thought more of your future than of their own wishes. You wouldn't want them to be sad."

George felt more and more downcast. "Now I've messed everything up again," he thought. He couldn't say a word.

"They're having a pretty hard time, and it seems you had something to do with it."

The fight! The broken dishes! George felt sick. He felt like crying again. But he fought back the tears.

"And let's see, wasn't there something else?" Brother Matthias hesitated.

"Sure," George said in a small voice. "I didn't want to go to school." He was fighting to keep back the tears.

Brother Matthias handed George a handkerchief. Then he turned to the window and started to close it.

"What's this?" Brother Matthias shook the heavy screen. "George, you've broken some of this wire netting loose. That's too bad, because it doesn't belong to you. It's school property. Now we'll have to get a man to repair it."

This was a new idea to George. He had never

thought about respecting other people's property when he was running around the streets. He felt worse than ever.

George managed to find his voice. "I don't want to hurt anybody. I guess I'm just no good." He hung his head.

"Well," said Brother Matthias with a big smile, "that's where you're wrong! Let me tell you something—something I want you to remember. Every boy is good—for something. That's why we run this school. We want to help boys find out just what it is they can do best. Lots of boys haven't had much of a chance. We try to give it to them. We want to give *you* a chance. But you must let us help you."

Brother Matthias talked so kindly and so firmly that George listened carefully. And he understood. He looked over at Brother Matthias. "Gee," thought George, "I guess he knows what he's talking about. If I could only be like Brother Matthias someday, maybe I wouldn't be all mixed up, the way I feel now."

"You know, George," Brother Matthias said, "Brother Dominic told me you didn't want anybody to get ahead of you. Well, the boys don't know that. You'll have to stick around here for a while if you're going to show them. How about it? Will you stay?"

"Sure!" George said. "I—I'll stay."

"Good!" said Brother Matthias. "By the way, I ought to tell you what my job is around here. I'm the prefect of discipline. That means I have to see that all the boys follow the rules."

George whistled in astonishment.

Brother Matthias threw back his head and laughed—a big hearty laugh. "That's right!" he said. "I have to decide whether a boy will be punished. It isn't easy, I can tell you!"

George spoke up. "You mean you're going to punish me?"

"Well," said Brother Matthias, "we won't tell Brother Dominic, because it would only make him sad. Suppose we forget all about this. How would that be?"

"That would be fine!" George thought again how nice Brother Dominic had been.

"But of course I'll expect you to follow the rules in the future," said Brother Matthias. "And the first rule is that you should be in bed right now. Come along!"

He put his hand on George's shoulder, and they started up the stairs. George thought, "Yes sir, I will—I sure will follow the rules."

"By the way," Brother Matthias went on, "I hear you're a pretty good baseball player. Why don't you come out to the playground after supper some evening? I usually hit a few flies to the boys."

George could hardly wait until tomorrow.

GEORGE CATCHES

Right after supper the next day George headed for the big play yard.

"Come on, Johnny," he said, as they pushed back from the long table in the dining room. "Let's get in some practice."

"You bet!" Johnny said.

They hurried along through the crowd of boys. George didn't mind all the strange faces now. He didn't feel left out when he saw the others joking and laughing. He had Johnny with him—and Brother Matthias had invited him to practice.

It had been a busy day for George, and his

head was swimming with the new things he had done. Up at five o'clock. Then to chapel for Mass before breakfast. Then to school—and it wasn't at all so bad as he had pictured it! He wasn't the only new boy, anyway. Two other boys had started today. Then to the shirtmaking shop where he was going to work every day. Then another game of baseball—and he had played catcher for the Brownies again. Why, he wouldn't have missed this for anything!

"Hurry up," Johnny said, "or there won't be any mitts left!"

On the best baseball field in the corner of the yard, boys of all ages were scrambling for the well-used baseball gloves that belonged to the school. Johnny and George got the last two.

The boys spread out over the field. There were seniors, as well as youngsters like Johnny and George.

And there came Brother Matthias with his bat and ball and glove. George thought about last night. Why, he might have been in terrible trouble if it hadn't been for Brother Matthias! George couldn't help feeling good as he watched the big man walk up to the diamond. He didn't look like a fearsome giant, the way he had last night. But he certainly was big.

The boys all shouted, "Knock one to me, Brother Matthias!"

Brother Matthias nodded and smiled. He tossed the ball up with his gloved hand and swung the bat with his right hand only.

Smack! The bat hit the battered old ball, and it arched high and far, deep into center field. One of the bigger boys ran back and caught it.

"Wow!" cried George. "Did you see that, Johnny? Look how far he hit that ball—and with only one hand!"

"You haven't seen anything yet," Johnny said. "Just you wait."

George had never imagined that anybody could hit a ball that far—even with *two* hands. "Maybe *I* can learn to hit it like that," he thought.

Brother Matthias swung his bat again. This time he hit the ball sky-high. It looked as though it would never come down. But there it was—heading straight for George and Johnny in short left field.

"Go ahead and take it, George!" shouted Johnny.

George circled around under the ball.

One of the older boys whistled and shouted, "Watch out for your head!"

At the last minute George stuck up his glove. *Thud!* The ball hit the glove so hard it almost knocked George down. He staggered, fumbled the ball, then grabbed it with both hands.

"Got it!" he crowed. He pulled off his glove, grabbed the ball with his left hand, wound up, and threw with all his might. It was a good throw, right to Brother Matthias.

George didn't mind a bit that most of the

boys were laughing at the way he had stumbled around. He hadn't dropped the ball.

He'd show them, just the way Brother Matthias had said. George pounded his glove and waited for another chance.

Brother Matthias hit the ball all over the field. George watched him, wishing he could hit a ball that hard—with *two* hands.

A bouncing grounder came out toward George and Johnny. George started for it.

"Hey, my turn," Johnny shouted.

George wanted very much to get it, but he stopped and Johnny caught it neatly.

"There are too many kids here," George complained to Johnny. "I bet I don't even get another chance!"

And he didn't. A few minutes later, when every boy had caught at least one ball, Brother Matthias waved to them to come in. Instantly all the boys set up a shout, "Over the fence! Over the fence, Brother Matthias!"

Brother Matthias smiled and nodded. Once more he tossed up the ball. He still held the bat with his right hand only. He seemed to swing easily. But he put all the force of his powerful body behind it.

Smack! Higher and farther than ever the ball soared. All the boys stood with open mouths, watching it. Straight toward deep center field it went—and disappeared over the fence!

"Hurray!" the boys shouted happily. Two of them scrambled over the fence to get the ball.

"Whew!" George whistled. He just stood there, watching where the ball had disappeared. "Someday I'm going to do that," he vowed. "I'm going to be the best batter there is!"

SCHOOLWORK VERSUS BASEBALL

"ROD, CAN YOU tell me what this word is?" Brother Herman wrote in flowing letters *m-e-a-l-s* on the blackboard. It was late summer of George's first year at St Mary's.

Rod looked at the word. His lips moved but he didn't say anything. He squirmed uncomfortably. The other boys in the classroom giggled. This was going to be fun.

Brother Herman rapped for order. "All right, then, can *you* tell me, George?"

George smiled broadly. He had seen the

word a thousand times on the front of Pop's restaurant. He'd show that Rod! "That's *meals!*" said George triumphantly. He grinned at Rod, and Rod frowned back at him. The other boys laughed.

"That'll do!" said Brother Herman. "Now, George, spell it for me."

But George was thinking about Rod. He looked quickly back at the word. Somehow he couldn't say the letters!

"Why—why—it's *meals,* that's all I know," he stammered.

Now the boys roared at George. Brother Herman rapped for order again. His black eyes flashed. "George, if you were as interested in spelling as you are in baseball, I'm sure you'd know this."

George gulped. "I can spell that word," he thought. "I just wasn't paying attention." He started to jump up and protest. Then he remembered what he had promised Brother Matthias. He would follow the rules!

"George and Rod, come up to the blackboard and write the word three times," Brother Herman said.

George rushed to the board, Rod right behind him. George picked up the chalk. "I'll just show them how to write," he decided. He looked at Brother Herman's smooth letters. Carefully he wrote. But his letters were all wiggly.

George tried harder. The chalk squeaked. The boys giggled. Still George's writing was shaky. Again he wrote the word. It made him angry that he couldn't do better—right in front of the whole class. He looked over at Rod's writing. It wasn't much better. But he went back to his seat muttering to himself.

"George and Rod will both have to work

hard if they expect to get a writing certificate," Brother Herman said. "Remember, the first boy to win a certificate gets a special prize."

"Well, I'll show 'em," George thought. "They won't get ahead of me." He was still angry over being laughed at when he was at the board.

The bell rang. The boys crowded out of the room. Rod walked past George and called to him, "Wait till the doubleheader this afternoon, stupid! The Brownies haven't got a chance!"

"Ho, ho!" George shouted. "We'll beat you the first game—we need only one for the championship!"

"That's right!" Johnny Peters shouted. "We won't even have to play a doubleheader."

Bob Young, the Brownies' first baseman, joined in. "We'll shut 'em out."

George, Johnny, and Bob walked together toward the industrial building.

"Do you think we can really beat them?" Johnny asked.

"Sure!" said George. "We need to win only the first game. Then we'll be champions of the Little Stars League! We'll show that Rod who knows how to play baseball. He thinks the Greenies will win easily."

"If they get lucky and win the first one, it will tie us in the league standing. Then we'll have another chance, and we'll surely win the second game," Bob said. "That will be just as good."

"You'd better hit some long balls this afternoon, George," said Johnny. "We've won a lot of games since you got on the team."

"Why, I'm going to hit one as far—as far as Brother Matthias can!" George got more and more excited as he thought about the games.

Bob burst out laughing. "Wow!" he said. "I'd like to see you do that."

Johnny couldn't help but laugh, too. Imagine anyone hitting the ball as far as Brother Matthias did!

"Don't laugh," George said. "I'm really going to hit one."

EXTRA WORK

In the shirtmaking shop each of the boys hurried to get started with his work. Johnny and Bob helped fold the finished shirts. It was George's job to lay out the cloth on the long tables.

Mr. Dean, who was in charge of the shop, helped George put out several bolts of heavy blue cloth. Then George began unrolling the bolts. He spread the cloth smoothly the length of the table. Then he spread another layer of cloth right on top of the first. Then another and another.

George looked at the clock. Still an hour before game time.

"Oops!" George cried. The cloth kept wrinkling as he tried to smooth it out. He jerked at it impatiently, but it only wrinkled worse. Instead of going back and smoothing out the wrinkles, George kept on unrolling the bolt. In his haste to finish, he covered up the wrinkled places with more cloth.

When he had enough layers of cloth laid out, George signaled to Mr. Dean. Mr. Dean took a pattern and marked, in white chalk on the top layer, the rough outlines of a shirt. Then two older boys with cutting machines started to cut the layers of cloth along these lines.

George went to the other side of the table. Once again he began laying out cloth. He was impatient because he couldn't seem to lay it straight. The more impatient he got, the more the cloth seemed to wrinkle. He jerked and pulled at the bolts. He looked at the clock. It seemed that it would never be time for the game.

Just then one of the boys using a cutting machine called out, "Mr. Dean, this whole pile is ruined. The cloth is all wrinkled."

Mr. Dean bustled over to the table. He went through the pile carefully. Half of the pieces were cut in the wrong places, because George had let the cloth stay wrinkled.

"George," said Mr. Dean, "what's the meaning of this? I told you how important it is to keep these layers smooth. Why, look what you're doing now! That cloth will all be wrong, too."

He hurried over to George. He pointed out the bad places in the cloth. "Now smooth that all out carefully," he said. "I've half a mind to keep you late to do extra work."

Keep him late? He'd miss the baseball game! Now George was angry. His temper had got the best of him. As Mr. Dean hustled back to look over the pattern pieces, George made a face at him. He stuck out his tongue. He put his thumbs in his ears and wiggled his fingers.

Bob Young saw him and started to laugh. But Bob stopped suddenly.

Through the door came Brother Matthias! The big man saw what George was doing. He looked surprised. He walked over to talk with Mr. Dean. Then the two men started slowly toward Mr. Dean's desk in the corner of the room. They had worried looks on their faces.

George was horrified. He set to work as fast as he could. He smoothed out all the wrinkles in the cloth before him. "Now what have I done?" he thought. "I certainly never wanted Brother Matthias to see me making that face!" His heart sank.

"Oh, George," called Brother Matthias, "will you come over here, please?"

With a long, sad face George walked over to Mr. Dean's desk.

"George," said Mr. Dean, "I'm afraid you'll

have to stay an extra hour today. You will lay out the material for tomorrow's work. I will help you, to see that it is done right. Your careless work today has ruined a great deal of cloth."

George cried out, "But what about the baseball game? Today we play for the championship! I have to play!"

Brother Matthias spoke up. "George, you know we have forty-three baseball teams here at the school. Six leagues. We'll have championship games on every field today. And all the boys who play have followed the rules and done their work properly. You know, you and I made an agreement about following the rules."

George hung his head. He felt miserable. He knew Brother Matthias was right. Still, he wanted more than anything else to play today.

"You see, George," Brother Matthias went

on, "we're trying to teach you to be a shirtmaker, so you can get a good job when you leave here. Work comes before play. And the best shirt-makers get the best jobs."

Desperately George spoke up. "I'll be the best shirtmaker you ever saw. Yes, sir, I will. But just let me play today!"

Brother Matthias couldn't help smiling. "You never do anything halfway, do you, George?" But he shook his head. "I'm sorry, son. We can't forget about it this time. You'll have to do as Mr. Dean says."

George wanted to shout that he wouldn't. But Brother Matthias just looked at him. George hesitated. Brother Matthias was his friend. And, much as he hated to, George would do as Brother Matthias said. He hung his head. "All right," he said in a small voice.

Brother Matthias walked to the door. He

paused. "George," he said, "you'll probably be out in time to get into a game."

But the extra hour was the longest George had ever spent.

GEORGE GETS A BIG HIT

After he had laid out carefully the last bolt of cloth, George rushed to the baseball field. There were Rod and the Greenies all shouting and slapping one another on the back. The Brownies were grouped over by their bench. They all looked very unhappy.

"What happened?" asked George.

"Aw, they beat us, 5–0," said Johnny. "What's the idea, getting into trouble today? We needed you!"

"Yeah," said Mario Serra, the second baseman. "Joe caught for us, and he hurt his finger again."

"Why'd you have to do that today?" Bob Young asked.

"Gee, I didn't mean to," George said. "May I catch the second game?"

"It's about time you got here," Brother Herman said as he hurried up. "Here's your glove. Now you Brownies get out on the field."

George let out a whoop and rushed for the plate. The Brownies had to win this game for the championship!

"Shoot it right across, Johnny," George shouted. He thumped his mitt. Johnny took a few warm-up pitches. Then the first Greenie batter came to the plate. The game was on!

For two and a half innings no one reached first base. Then in the last of the third Mario got a walk. It was George's turn to hit. He grabbed the bat. "Now I'll show 'em," he thought. "I'll hit one so far they'll never find it."

Brother Herman hurried over. He was acting as coach for both teams—and umpire as well. "George," he said, "lay down a bunt. Then you'll move Mario down to second, into scoring position."

"A bunt?" George was startled. He wanted to hit hard. He never had bunted before.

Brother Herman was already back behind Rod, ready to call balls and strikes. George walked to the plate, mumbling to himself. "A bunt! Aw, gee!"

The Greenie pitcher fired the ball over the plate. George stuck out his bat, trying to roll the ball slowly down the first-base line. But he hit under the ball. It popped lazily straight up in the air. Rod grabbed it quickly.

"There's an easy out!" Rod crowed.

George gave him an angry look and walked back to the bench.

Someone sat down beside him. It was Brother Matthias. George was tongue-tied.

Brother Matthias smiled and patted George on the back. "Too bad, George," he said. "I guess you wanted to hit a long ball, eh?"

George nodded.

"Well, just remember, baseball is a team game," said Brother Matthias. "A good batter must know how to bunt when it's necessary."

Just then Johnny smashed a ground ball through the infield into center field. He stopped at first base, and Mario went to second.

"You see, George," said Brother Matthias, "your team could have had a run now, if you had been able to advance Mario to second. Mario could have scored from second on that single."

George nodded again.

"You have the makings of a pretty good baseball player," Brother Matthias went on.

George could hardly believe his ears. He sat up straighter.

"On that bunt, you just took your eyes off the ball," said Brother Matthias. "Remember, the first rule of batting is: Keep your eyes on the ball."

Jack Frye, third baseman for the Brownies, struck out. That made two down. Bob Young came to bat.

"There's a lot to learn about baseball," Brother Matthias said. "Would you like me to show you a few things in your spare time?"

George nearly jumped off the bench. "Yes, sir!" he said, grinning from ear to ear.

Just then Bob Young grounded out to the first baseman. The Brownies took the field.

George thumped his mitt. Brother Matthias wasn't really angry with him. And he was going to give him some tips on baseball!

Neither team scored, right up to the last half of the last inning. Then with two out for the Brownies, Mario went all the way to second on an error.

George jumped up. Now was his chance!

"All right, George," said Brother Herman. "Hit away this time!"

George got set at the plate. He shuffled his feet until they felt good and solid. He held the bat ready. "Watch that ball!" he said to himself.

The pitcher threw—straight over the plate and about shoulder-high. Watching the ball like a hawk, George swung with all his might.

Sock! He connected solidly. The ball flew on a line far into right field. It went right between the center fielder and the right fielder, and rolled all the way to the next baseball diamond.

By the time the right fielder got it, George

had rounded third base. He crossed the plate, grinning broadly. It was a home run.

"Wow, what a wallop!" said Rod, standing sadly at the plate.

All the other Brownies crowded around, shouting and laughing.

"We win, 2–0!" Johnny shouted. "You really hit that one, George!"

"I certainly did!" George said happily. At that Mario burst out laughing. But George wasn't bragging. He was just happy.

A CURE FOR TEMPER

IT WAS EARLY in 1905—nearly three years later. Brother Herman and Brother Matthias sat discussing the St. Mary's baseball leagues for the coming summer.

"Well, that about settles it," Brother Herman said. "It looks as though we'll have forty teams in five leagues."

Brother Matthias sighed. "I wish we had more equipment. But I guess we're doing pretty well to have as much as we do."

Brother Herman grinned. "We ought to get a

left-handed catcher's mitt for George Ruth. He doesn't want to do anything but catch."

"On which team do you plan to play him this year?" asked Brother Matthias.

"Well, he's getting a little too good for the boys his own age. Let's see, he's ten now. Maybe he ought to play with the OK's—in the twelve-year-old league."

"Good idea! It'll do him good to get more competition. Otherwise he might get too much of a swelled head."

"I was afraid to say that because I thought he was a special pet of yours." Brother Herman grinned mischievously.

"You know better than to think I'd favor one boy more than another," Brother Matthias said, laughing. "Besides, I've seen you giving him special instruction, too." It was Brother Matthias's turn to grin.

"He's a good prospect for the school team when he gets a little older. And I try to teach all the boys the sound fundamentals of baseball."

Brother Matthias thought a minute. "You're right that I've taken a special interest in him. He was very lonely when he got here. And he's likely to feel terribly unhappy if we don't keep his interest aroused."

Brother Herman laughed. "It's not hard to keep him interested in baseball."

"That's right. And, you know, I've seldom seen a boy with such a good eye. It's hard to fool him when he's at bat. He's big for his age, and he's strong as can be. But he still must learn to control his temper."

"Let's try him out on the OK's," Brother Herman said. He looked up at the clock. "We'd better get along and check over the equipment."

The two brothers went out to the big empty

play yard. They looked over the bats, balls, and gloves. They counted the stuffed canvas bases that would be used on the diamonds. They laid aside the equipment to be mended.

They stood looking over the yard in the chill March wind.

The bell sounded. Shop work was over for the day. The boys soon began rushing out the door to play in the yard. There was a shout from one of the boys. He came rushing over to the brothers. In spite of the cold, he was wearing just a shirt with his denim overalls. It was George, and he was bubbling with excitement.

"Isn't it time to start baseball?" he shouted. "Won't you bat out some balls, Brother Matthias—or you, Brother Herman?"

Brother Matthias held up his hand. "Quietly, quietly, George!" said the big man. "What do you think, Brother Herman?"

"You go ahead. I must referee a soccer game."
Brother Herman strode off to the far end of the
field. George rushed to get ball, bat, and glove.
He was anxious to begin playing baseball again.
He had missed it during the winter.

GEORGE AND ROD COLLIDE

"Let's have a little pepper game to loosen up,"
said Brother Matthias. "Shouldn't you have
your sweater, George? You'll catch cold."

"Oh, no, I'm too tough for that," George said
with a grin.

"Don't be too sure," said Brother Matthias.
"You know, an athlete has to keep himself in
good condition."

"Oh?" said George.

"Certainly. He has to watch his diet and get
plenty of sleep."

George nodded.

"That applies to you, too, George, even though I know you're pretty strong," Brother Matthias went on. He smiled at George. His eyes twinkled. "I've heard that you're seldom ready for sleep at lights-out. Just don't forget to take care of yourself if you want to be an athlete. That's important."

"Gee," George said. "I never thought of that."

"Try to remember it. Well, that's enough lecturing for today! Let's have that pepper game."

George took his position only a short distance away.

Brother Matthias hit short grounders and sharp liners. George scooped them up, and he pitched back to Brother Matthias as fast as he could. Back and forth went the ball. Finally George let a grounder go through his legs.

"Keep down, keep down!" Brother Matthias advised, as George came running back with the ball. "Always try to get right in front of the ball if you can. And keep low. Then you can block the ball if it takes a bad bounce."

"I'll try it," George said.

Brother Matthias hit the ball first to the left, then to the right. George hurried one way, then the other. He tried to do what Brother Matthias said. It was hard work—but he loved it. Each time he caught the ball he felt better. Another whole season of baseball was starting!

As the pepper game continued, Brother Matthias and George called back to one another.

"Why do you insist on playing catcher?" Brother Matthias asked. "You know, there aren't any left-handed catchers in the big leagues. And we haven't even got a mitt for you."

George caught a short fly. He sent the ball back to Brother Matthias. "What's wrong with a left-handed catcher?" he asked.

"Well, a great many batters are right-handed," said Brother Matthias. "They stand directly in the way of a left-handed catcher's throw."

"Aw, that doesn't bother me," George said.

"Besides, I've tried other positions. But catching's best. Why, I get to be in on every play!"

Brother Matthias smiled. "You're right, there," he said. "But if you're going to be a good catcher, you must learn to make a quick throw."

"How do you mean?" George asked.

"Here, I'll show you." Brother Matthias caught the ball. "You haven't got time to do this," Brother Matthias said as he leaned way back with his arm extended full length.

"Instead, you've got to do this." Brother Matthias crouched like a catcher. He cocked his arm. The ball in his hand was pulled no farther back than his ear. He threw the ball to George in a quick snap throw.

"Gee!" said George. "I see what you mean. But I like to wind up and really throw it!"

Brother Matthias laughed. "Yes, I know you like to do everything in a big way. But to

88

be a good catcher you've got to learn that snap throw."

George took the ball. He cocked his arm several times. It seemed very awkward. He didn't see how he could throw with any power if he followed Brother Matthias's advice. Still he was determined to learn how.

"Hey, can I play too?" came a shout. Rod rushed up. Right behind him came Johnny Peters. They both ran to get gloves.

"Certainly, come and join us," Brother Matthias said.

George frowned. He was having such a good time—and learning so much about the game! Now Rod would interfere. Johnny was all right, but Rod was always making trouble. "Aw, do they have to play?" George complained.

"Well, son, it takes more than one player to make a team," Brother Matthias reminded him.

The three boys lined up in front of the big man. Now the pepper game started in earnest. Back and forth, back and forth went the ball. The boys fielded and threw as fast as they could.

Brother Matthias hit a grounder right between George and Rod. Both boys started for it. Rod bumped George aside and grabbed the ball before George could recover.

"Hey, it was my turn!" George shouted.

"You'll have to hurry, stupid," Rod said in a low voice so that Brother Matthias couldn't hear. George thumped his mitt and glared at Rod.

Johnny caught a line drive and threw to Brother Matthias. Back came the ball—right between George and Rod again.

"Got it!" both boys shouted together, as they dove for the ball. They ran into each other so hard that they both fell to the ground. The ball trickled past.

George tried to jump up, but Rod was lying on him. He gave Rod a shove. Rod rolled over and took a swing at George. George dove at him. In an instant they were wrestling and hitting in a mad scramble.

Suddenly they felt themselves jerked to their feet. Brother Matthias had both boys by their collars—one in each hand. "Here, here, what's all this?" he said. "This is no way to have a friendly game of baseball."

"I didn't do anything," Rod said innocently.

"Well, I did!" shouted George. "He's been after me ever since I came to this school. I'm going to show him he can't get away with it."

"How about it, Rod?" asked Brother Matthias.

"Aw, he's just stupid, and I told him so," Rod grumbled without thinking.

"Well, well," Brother Matthias said, "it looks to me as though you're both at fault. Do you want to shake hands now, or do you want to go on fighting?"

"I want to fight him," shouted George, his temper thoroughly aroused.

"How about you, Rod?"

Rod gulped. He didn't really want to fight. But he didn't want to back down. "Aw, I'll fight him," he said.

"All right, boys," said Brother Matthias. "We can't have you brawling out here on the field.

There's just one way to settle this—with boxing gloves—in a fair fight."

A LAUGHING MATTER

Brother Matthias went ahead to get the gloves.

Johnny trotted along with George. "You can beat him, George," he said. "He's asked for it. He's always making trouble."

But George wasn't happy. He was worried. "What will Brother Matthias think?" he wondered.

"Now I bet Brother Matthias won't coach me anymore," he said sadly to Johnny. "I always have to go and mess things up."

"Don't worry," said Johnny. "Brother Matthias isn't so dumb. He knows Rod has been making things tough for you."

George felt a little better. Maybe Johnny was right. Still, he shouldn't have fought with

Rod. But he couldn't let Rod shove him around, either.

The boys on the playground had heard about the fight. They rushed to the play hall, put a couple of chairs some distance apart in the center of the hall, and gathered around anxiously.

"Let's have plenty of room here in the center," Brother Matthias said, as he put the big boxing gloves on George and Rod. Then he looked at the two and added: "Who knows? We might find a good prospect for the boxing team out of this fight."

He brought the boys to the center of the open space. Rod and George glared at each other. "I'll flatten him," thought George, gritting his teeth. "He can't make fun of me!"

"Now, let's have a clean, fair fight," said Brother Matthias. "Two rounds. Ready? Go!"

Hardly were the words out of his mouth when

George rushed at Rod, hitting out wildly—left, right, then left again.

There were excited shouts all around him. "Come on, George!"

"Stop him, Rod!" others shouted.

The chunky Rod backed away a little. George's blows fell short, but he waded right in. He swung hard with his right. Rod blocked the blow with his gloves. Still George kept hitting with all his might. One of his blows caught Rod on the side of his head. In return Rod poked George in the nose. The gloves were so big and padded that it didn't hurt George—but it stung. He struck right back, and caught Rod on the nose. Then they stood in the center of the ring, each hitting as hard as he could.

Gradually George forced Rod to back up. Now Rod was trying hard to block George's swings.

"I've got him," George thought. He charged in, raining blows on Rod's shoulders and arms. Rod kept backing away. George's friends shouted louder and louder.

"Time!" Brother Matthias called. "End of round one."

Rod and George sat on their chairs, puffing and panting. The other boys shouted advice.

"Keep after him, George," called Johnny.

Brother Matthias talked to Rod a minute. Then he came over to George. "Feeling all right?" he asked. He looked George over.

"Sure, I'm fine," George said, puffing. "That Rod had better watch out."

"Time!" called Brother Matthias again.

George jumped up. He rushed toward Rod again. He started swinging. "My gosh, these gloves feel heavy!" thought George. His arms felt like lead. He jabbed hard with his left,

then his right. He was so tired he stepped back a bit.

Rod moved in. George lifted his hands to block Rod's blows. But he was too slow. Rod caught him right on the chin. George stumbled backward and sat down, hard.

George looked so surprised that some of the boys started to laugh. He jumped up and charged at Rod. He took a wild swing—and missed. He swung so hard he spun completely around. Now more of the boys were laughing.

Rod charged. He struck blindly at George— and he missed. He almost fell down! Now the boys laughed harder than ever.

Puffing and panting, George charged in again. This time the big glove connected with Rod's head. He stumbled and sat down. Wildly he jumped up again.

George and Rod stood glaring at each other

for a second. Then they both swung at once, as hard as they could. The blows whistled through the air and missed! George and Rod both spun around with the force of their blows. They were so exhausted that they lost their balance. *Thud!* They sat down hard on the floor. There they stayed, each looking into the other's surprised face. Neither could move.

"Ha, ha, ha!" roared the boys.

George glared around angrily. Then he turned back to Rod. He looked so funny just sitting there! "I must look funny, too," George thought. Suddenly he burst out laughing. He then realized that Rod was laughing, too.

Brother Matthias was grinning. He helped the boys up. "I guess the fight's over," he said. Then he called out loudly, "I declare the official verdict—a draw!"

All the boys cheered and shouted and laughed.

"Come on, boys, and shake hands," said Brother Matthias.

George was tired, but he was feeling much better. He wasn't angry at Rod any longer. He pushed back his long dark hair and stuck out his hand to Rod. Rod smiled and stuck out his hand, too.

"I guess there's room enough on the baseball field for both of you boys, isn't there?" Brother Matthias said.

"Sure!" said George.

"You bet," panted Rod.

Then the other boys rushed in. They surrounded George and Rod, laughing and shouting excitedly.

"Some fight!" said Johnny, slapping George on the back.

"Ha, ha, ha!" Mario laughed. "I never had so much fun!"

"Come on, let's have those gloves," Brother Matthias said. He untied them from George's hands.

"I don't think I'll try out for the boxing team," George said. "I think I'd better stick to baseball!"

GEORGE GETS TWO SURPRISES

"COME ON, FELLOWS!" shouted George. "Let's stop 'em. Come on!"

There came the ball. But it was right over the middle of the plate! The batter swung hard and lined a safe hit to left field. Another Cub runner crossed the plate.

George groaned as he stood at the plate and watched the OK fielder go after the ball.

"Watch my signals, Billy," he shouted. Billy Pazdan was the second OK pitcher. Jim Lutz had already been knocked out of the box.

Billy got the ball. He got ready to pitch to the next Cub batter. George watched the Cub runner on first. He was taking a long lead. George signaled to his pitcher and first baseman. He wanted them to be prepared.

Billy wound up and threw. It was a wide pitch, but it was right where George wanted it. He pulled off his mitt, seized the ball with his left hand, and snapped it to Del Wilms, the OK first baseman. Too late the Cub runner dove for the bag. Del tagged him out.

"At last!" George shouted. He took off his chest protector. "Six runs behind! Let's get some ourselves."

"Nice play at first," Billy said as he came to the bench. "Whew! I can't seem to pitch today, for some reason."

George picked up a bat. "Let's get some runs!" he called again as he walked to the plate. But all

George could do was hit foul balls. He gave the ball a long ride toward right field, but outside the foul line. Ball after ball he hit foul. "What's the matter with me today?" he wondered. "Why do I pull it around like that? I'll have to ask Brother Matthias." Finally he struck out.

George shook his head. "Start it off, Billy," he said as he handed over the bat. But the OK's went out in order.

As the game went on, the Cubs' score mounted. Billy was knocked out of the box. Tom Padget came in from third to pitch an inning. Then Jack Mishler came in from right field to pitch. The score was 13–0! Still the Cubs lined out safe hits.

George talked and pleaded and shouted. The next Cub batter drove a triple nearly out of the field. George threw his glove high in the air. "Ha, ha, ha!" he roared. "What's the matter

with you pitchers today? Why don't you go back
to the Brownies?"

Jack and the other OK's looked surprised.
Then as George kept on laughing, they shouted,
"Aw, shut up! What's the big idea?"

But George wasn't to be stopped. He had
tried hard to rally the team. Nothing seemed
to work. Now it struck him as funny, the way
the Cubs were whacking almost every pitch, the
way the balls whistled off the Cub bats.

"Come on, Jack," George called. "Where's he going to hit it this time?"

Angrily Jack pitched to the next batter.

Crack! went the bat. It was another base hit, right through the box.

"Ha, ha, ha!" George shouted.

"Well, George, I know you have a sense of humor, but don't you think it's a little out of place now?"

George turned at the voice. It was Brother Matthias. And he wasn't smiling.

George didn't know what to say. He sputtered, "Why—why—those pitchers are getting knocked all over the lot."

"You're showing pretty poor sportsmanship, don't you think?"

"Aw, gee, I didn't mean it that way," said George sadly. Why was he always doing the wrong thing?

"Well, suppose you just go out there to the pitcher's mound and see what you can do."

George gulped. "Me?" he faltered. "Why, I can't pitch. I—I'm a catcher."

Now Brother Matthias smiled. "You seem to know a lot about pitching. Go ahead. See what you can do."

George walked slowly out to the mound, shaking his head. Now it was the turn of the other OK's to laugh. George didn't like it. "I guess I've got it coming, though," he thought.

He traded gloves with Jack Mishler. "Gee, I'm sorry, Jack," he said. "I didn't mean to make fun of you. But that score—"

"Maybe it is kind of funny after all," Jack said. "I'll be glad to catch. It's safer!"

George gulped. He tried standing on the pitcher's mound. He wound up a few times. "This is a little awkward," he thought. "But I don't have to make those snap throws! I can really cut loose and throw the ball. And since I'm pitching, I'll show them something."

He fired the ball with all his might to Jack. He took several more practice throws. This wasn't bad after all! "I'll show 'em. I'll get those Cubs out!"

The next Cub batter came to the plate. It didn't look so easy now, but George wound up and pitched. Straight for the plate it went. *Smack!* It hit the catcher's glove before the batter could move the bat off his shoulder.

"Strike one!" called the umpire.

Ball after ball George threw with all the force of his strong left arm. One after another he struck out the next three Cub batters.

The OK's rushed to the bench, cheering and laughing.

Jack pulled off his mitt. He wrung his hand.

"Wow!" he said to George. "You nearly tore my hand off."

Brother Matthias shook his head. He smiled. "I tried to teach you a lesson, George," he said. "But I guess I learned something myself. It looks as though the OK's have a new pitcher."

"I really like pitching," George said happily. Then he stopped smiling. "But I'm sorry about laughing that way. I—I guess I just didn't think. I—I won't do it again."

"That's fine, George."

George hesitated. "Brother Matthias, there's something wrong with my hitting today. I keep hitting them all foul. Could—could you help me straighten it out?"

Brother Matthias smiled at George. "Are you sure you don't know more about hitting than I do?" Then he laughed. "I shouldn't make fun of you, either. Of course I'll help, if I can."

"Tonight after supper?" George asked quickly.

"You're a determined fellow. All right, tonight it is! You go ahead to the play yard as soon as you've finished eating. I'll meet you there, and we'll see if we can find out what your trouble is."

THE AWARDS

It was a few days later. Brother Herman rapped for order in the schoolroom. "Today," he said, "I want to announce the results of our pen-and-ink writing test. I am glad to say that one of our students has qualified for the writing certificate."

The boys all looked around at one another. They wondered who had won.

"Since he's first in the class to win, I have also another prize—a medal. The boy who qualified is—George Ruth."

There was a buzz of excitement. Mario Serra said to Johnny Peters, "Can you imagine that! I

thought George thought only about baseball."

George grinned a big grin. He had been working hard to win that certificate. He hadn't told anyone how hard he had practiced. He had worked at it ever since that day he and Rod had been sent to the blackboard. And now he had shown everybody that he didn't do everything wrong.

"Come on up, George," said Brother Herman.

George shoved back his mop of hair. He walked to the front. He wished he had known about this two days ago. He had been home for his regular visit. He could have told Mom and Pop. Maybe it would have cheered them up. They still weren't having an easy time.

"All right, George, here's your writing certificate. And here's your prize for being first to win one. Let's hope the rest of the class will not be far behind."

George took the certificate and the medal. "Thanks, Brother Herman." He started for his seat.

"Just a moment, just a moment! I think we should have a demonstration."

George stopped. He turned red.

"Go to the board and write out our song for us," Brother Herman said.

Slowly George walked to the board. "This isn't like playing baseball," he thought. "How can I write up here in front of the whole class?"

He seized a piece of chalk. "I guess I've got to do it," he thought. He started copying off the stanza that was always written on the side board. Smoothly and carefully he put down the words. Without knowing it, he stuck out his tongue. He worked his mouth, silently pronouncing the letters as he wrote. He didn't realize how funny he looked.

Some of the boys giggled.

George got a little flustered, but he wrote on. He finished with a flourish. There it was, in smooth, flowing writing:

Boys, be up and doing,
For the day's begun.
Soon will come the noontide,

Then the set of sun.
At your task toil bravely
Till your work is done.

"That's fine, George," said Brother Herman. "Now the rest of you can follow a good example. Class dismissed."

Johnny clapped loudly. So did the others. George walked out with them, his face still red.

Rod called out in a shrill, high voice, "Write me a letter, Georgie-boy!"

Everyone roared at that. George chased Rod. But he wasn't angry. He didn't mind Rod's teasing him now that they were friends.

"I will—if you'll let me play your bass drum some time," shouted George, clapping Rod on the back. Rod carried the bass drum in the school band. And George loved the *thump, thump* Rod made when he pounded the big drum.

Johnny caught up with Rod and George. "Say, George, I hear you're going to be a pitcher. I wish you were still on our team."

"Johnny," said George, "will you help me learn to pitch a curve? All I can do now is throw the ball hard."

"Sure!" Johnny said. "Any time."

SCHOOL CHAMPIONS

IT WAS FIVE years later. A huge crowd of boys gathered on the number one baseball diamond in the play yard. Everyone was chattering about the big game. It was the game for the school championship, between the two top teams of the senior league.

"Who's going to win?" Rod asked.

"The White Sox, of course," Johnny said. "With George pitching and batting, the Pirates haven't got a chance."

Rod whistled. "Don't you be too sure! It'll

be a close game. Besides, George isn't going to pitch this afternoon."

"Why?" Mario asked.

"He pitched yesterday. Brother Herman's going to start Billy Pazdan."

"You wait," Johnny advised. "I bet George will be pitching before the game's over!"

Out on the field George was back at his old job—catching. "Come on, Billy, fire it right in here," he shouted. Billy threw his last warm-up pitch, and the game was on.

First up for the Pirates was Tom Padget, George's old teammate on the OK's. Billy walked him on four straight pitches.

George went out to talk to Billy. He grinned at him. "Don't make it too easy for them, Billy. Fire it over. Let them make the mistakes!"

The next two batters hit easy pop flies. Then Joey Jacobs came to bat. He was the Pirates' heavy hitter, the first baseman. He slammed the ball far down the right-field line for a triple, and the Pirates led, 1–0.

There the score stood for four innings. George got up to bat twice. But he walked both times. Jim Lutz, the pitcher, another old OK player, wasn't taking any chances.

In the first half of the fifth inning the Pirates got another run. Joey Jacobs got a walk this time. Bill Padget, Tom's brother, was safe on Bobby Horn's error at shortstop. And Lutz hit a clean single to score Jacobs.

"Come on, fellows, it's time we scored," shouted George when the other side was out. He was first up to bat. He waited until the count was three balls and two strikes. Then he hit a long line drive for a double. Del Wilms, playing at first for the White Sox, got an infield single. The White Sox had men on first and third, with nobody out.

But the next three batters were easy outs, and the Pirates still led, 2–0.

In the top of the seventh the Pirates filled the bases on a single, an error, and a walk. There were two out.

George went out to the pitcher's mound. Del Wilms came over from first. They wanted to talk to Billy. Joey Jacobs was up to bat again.

Brother Herman walked out to join them. "You take over, George," he said. "You're getting a little tired, Billy. You play third base, and let Slim Morgan catch."

Cheers went up from the spectators as George took his practice throws. They liked to see him pitch. George stretched and threw. When you pitched you had to throw so differently from when you caught. George wasn't quite ready when the umpire called time.

He couldn't seem to throw to Jacobs where

he wanted the ball to go. He threw three times, all outside. Then he got a curve over, and Jacobs fouled it on the ground. "Now I've got him," George thought. He tried to throw the same curve. But it was wide, for a ball. Jacobs got a walk to first base—and a run was forced across the plate! The Pirates led, 3–0.

Now the Pirate fans shouted and clapped.

"Gee," Mario said, "it looks bad for George!"

"Just you wait," said Johnny. "He'll settle down."

George got ready to pitch to Bill Padget. "I've got to get him out," he thought. He threw a fast ball with all his might. Bill swung. But he hit under the ball. It popped lazily into George's mitt! The side was out, with three men left on base.

"Let's get started!" George said to Slim Morgan, first at bat for the White Sox in the bottom of the seventh. Slim nodded. He hit a ball to deep shortstop, and just beat the throw to first.

Then George came to bat. "Jim's going to be a little worried, after that single," he thought. "I'll watch that first ball he throws!"

There it came, not too hard, right over the plate.

George slammed it far into right field. It dropped for a safe hit. George ran with all his might. He wound up at third, with a triple, and Slim scored easily. It was 3–1 in favor of the Pirates now.

George scored when the Pirate catcher let a ball get away from him, and the score was 3–2. There it stayed for the next two innings.

In the top of the eighth and the top of the ninth, George struck out the other side each time! He was feeling good now, and he threw the ball just where he wanted it.

"Six strikeouts in a row!" shouted Johnny. "What did I tell you? Boy, that George can really pitch!"

"But they're still behind," Rod said.

In the bottom of the ninth, Jardin and Kelly both grounded out for the White Sox.

"Hey, Slim, this is our last chance," George called. "They'll be looking for you to swing hard. Why not lay down a bunt? How about that, Brother Herman?"

Brother Herman nodded. "Think you can do it, Slim? George is right. You may be able to catch the Pirates off guard."

"Just you watch!"

On the first pitch Slim trickled the ball down the third-base line. Tom Padgett was playing way back. By the time he fielded the ball, Slim had run across first base safely.

It was George's turn to bat.

"I've really got to hit now," George said to himself.

All the boys shouted as he walked to the plate. They brought out tin cans filled with rocks. They shook the cans wildly as they cheered. It was "Come on, George!" from one side, and "Strike him out, Joe!" from the other. The clatter was deafening.

George took a couple of practice swings. "Keep your eye on the ball," he told himself, "and take a nice level swing. If I could only hit one as far as Brother Matthias does!"

There came the ball—just where he wanted it: about waist-high, a little outside the plate. George stepped forward and swung with all his might.

Crack! He hit the ball. He swung all the way around, so hard he almost toppled over.

He recovered quickly and dashed for first base. Ahead of him he saw the ball soaring far and high. It—it was disappearing over the fence! It was a home run, and the White Sox had won, 4–3.

George trotted around the bases. As he crossed home plate all the White Sox grabbed him and thumped him on the back.

George caught sight of Brother Matthias. "I

tried to hit one just the way you do," he said. "I've been wanting to do that for a long time."

"You picked the right time," said Brother Matthias with a smile.

THE ACADEMY GAME

"HEY, GEORGE, WAIT'LL you hear!" Johnny Peters shouted, as he ran out the door of the main building one day the following year.

"Did you hear about the game?" George asked.

"No," said Johnny, "but—but I'm going to leave here." He smiled.

"You're kidding! You're not twenty-one yet."

"I'm going home," Johnny announced. "My dad's got a good job now, and I'm going home to live."

"Gee!" said George. "That—that's wonderful. Wish I could go, too."

"What's this about a game?" Johnny asked.

George was thinking about Johnny's going home. Home! He wondered if he'd ever go. "The game? Oh, yes. St. Mary's is going up to Emmitsburg, Maryland, to play the freshman team at the academy. Next week. The band's going and everything."

"I'd love to see you pitch. That will be the toughest team you've played so far."

"I guess they're pretty good," said George. "But we're not so bad, either."

"You said it! The way you've been striking out about fifteen a game! And knocking the cover off the ball!"

George laughed. "Remember what Brother Matthias always says. We've got eight other players on the team."

Johnny laughed too. "Well, I've got to hurry and tell the rest of the fellows about my going. I'll say good-bye to you later." He ran off.

George stood thinking a minute. Then he walked into the main building. He hadn't seen Mom and Pop very often during the years he had been at St. Mary's. Maybe they were getting along better now. Maybe he, too, could go home.

Impulsively George walked toward the superintendent's office. He met Brother Paul coming out. Brother Paul had taken the place of Brother Dominic.

"Why, hello, George," he said. "What can I do for you?"

George knit his forehead. He looked very serious. "I was just talking to Johnny—and do you think I'll ever be able to go home for good—before I'm twenty-one?"

"Well, George, I've always hoped you could. But I haven't talked with your parents recently. Let me think." He paused a minute. "How would this be? I know it isn't time for your yearly visit. But why don't you go home today and come back tomorrow and tell me about it?"

George brightened up. "I'd like that!"

"All right. Come see me here tomorrow at about this time."

"Thanks, Brother Paul!"

"Just one more thing, George," said Brother Paul with a smile: "I hope you won't leave for good before you pitch against the academy."

THE TEAM DEPENDS ON YOU

Twenty-four hours later George walked into Brother Paul's office. Brother Matthias was there, too. George was looking very sad.

"Come on, sit down and tell us about it, George," said Brother Paul.

"I guess I'll never be going home to stay," George said. "I'll have to stay here until I'm twenty-one."

"Why, what's the matter, son?" asked Brother Matthias.

"Well," said George. "Mom and Pop are still having a pretty hard time. They still can't look after me the way they'd like. They'd love to have me with them, but they think it's better for me if I stay here. And—and Pop told me—he doesn't think Mom's ever going to get well."

Tears stood in his eyes. He looked down at the floor.

"I'm very sorry, son. And I hope you're wrong about your mother." Brother Paul spoke softly.

"I guess I was never much good to them,"

George mourned. "I just made them a lot of trouble. And they had to send me here."

Brother Matthias was worried. "George, there's one thing you can do," he said. "You've made a good record here. You just go on doing that. You mustn't give up."

Brother Paul said, "George, you can make your parents proud of you—that is a great deal you can do for them. You can make us proud of you, too."

"I—I really love it here," George said. "Gee, you ought to know that! But I'm always making mistakes—losing my temper and—"

"Everyone does once in a while, George," said Brother Paul. "We just hope you've learned not to make too many mistakes!"

"Son," said Brother Matthias, "do you remember that day when you wrinkled up all the cloth in the tailor shop?"

"Why—why, yes."

"You told me you were going to be the best shirtmaker going. Well, Mr. Dean tells me you *are* about the best worker he has in the shop. You should be proud of that."

"Yes," said Brother Paul, "if you're determined to do something, you can do it. You've proved that. You've proved that you're a boy who can overcome handicaps. You can be a good citizen when you leave here."

George felt a little better. Yes, he *had* worked hard at his tailoring.

"You must remember, of course," said Brother Paul, "that we have pretty strict rules here. Out in the world it's different. There you must follow your own rules. It's up to you."

"I'll tell you what," said Brother Matthias, "I think we can arrange for you to do outside work in a tailor shop next year. You could earn some money that way. And you'd be ready for a really fine job when you leave here."

Brother Paul nodded. "I think that could be managed."

"Good!" said Brother Matthias. "And now,

George, you cheer up. Remember," he said with a smile, "you have an important ball game to pitch next week."

"Aw, gee," said George. "I love baseball, but I guess Mom and Pop wouldn't think much of it."

"George," said Brother Matthias, "you have something else to remember. Everybody on the team is depending on you. Everybody in the school expects St. Mary's to play a good game next Saturday. And you can't let them down."

"I—I never thought of that," George said. Why, he'd *have* to play—and do his very best!

"Think it over, George," said Brother Paul as George got up to leave. "I know you're going to feel better."

George walked slowly across the play yard. He walked into the quiet chapel. He tried to get his thoughts straight as he prayed. He still felt a little mixed up inside, but everything was beginning to look brighter.

A WONDERFUL TIME

The St. Mary's band marched smartly across the baseball field. It was the following Saturday, at the academy in Emmitsburg, Maryland, fifty miles from Baltimore. Few of the boys had ever been so far from home. The boys in the band were playing their best. They wanted to show that St. Mary's had as good a band as any school.

On the sideline benches George and the rest of the team waited for the game to begin. George always got a thrill watching the band. He watched Rod thump away on the bass drum. "If I weren't pitching, I'd like to be beating that drum," George thought.

"How do you feel, George?" Brother Matthias

leaned over to talk to him. "Ready to shut them out?"

George grinned. "We'll give them a battle," he promised. "I feel great!"

George had been thinking a lot about his visit home, and about his talk with Brother Paul and Brother Matthias. Why, he was lucky to be at St. Mary's! And he *would* make his family proud of him—and all the brothers at the school as well. He wouldn't give up.

"I guess I'm not so badly off," George thought. "Why, lots of the boys at St. Mary's are orphans and never even had a home."

All right! If he couldn't ever go home—if he was on his own—he'd show the world what he could do. "And right now, I've got to pitch a baseball game," he thought. "If I could only do *that* the rest of my life!"

The band paraded once more around the

field, then marched up into the big wooden stands. Rod and Mario sat together. Rod put his drum in the aisle. Mario stuck his flute in his pocket.

A man sat down behind them. "What game is this?" he asked. "I came to watch the university play the academy team."

"Oh, that's later," said Rod. "Our school is playing the academy freshmen in the first game."

"Well," said the man, "I guess I'm too early. I came to watch the college boys. I hear they have some good men. They might move into the big leagues someday."

Mario spoke up. "You just watch our team," he said. "George Ruth is the best pitcher around, and the best batter, too. And then there are Joey Jacobs and—"

"I suppose I might as well watch," the man interrupted.

"Come on, George!" Rod shouted as the St. Mary's boys took the field.

George threw a few practice balls to Slim Morgan, who was catching. His arm felt good.

"All set?" called Slim. George nodded.

"Batter up!" called the umpire.

The first academy batter stepped into the box. He was only about five feet tall. "I hope I can put the ball where I want it," George thought. "I'll surprise him."

He took a long windup. He stepped forward and let the ball go with all his strength. It streaked for the plate with blinding speed, a pitch just inside the strike zone.

"Strike one!" called the umpire.

"Atta boy, George!" Slim shouted as he fired the ball back.

"That's the way to pitch!" cried the other St. Mary's players.

The academy boy got set for the next pitch. "Now in close," George thought. He threw again, just as hard. This time the ball crossed the plate on the inside corner. The batter jumped back, thinking the ball might hit him.

"Strike two!"

George grinned as he caught the ball from Slim. If only he could keep this up!

The batter pounded the plate with his bat. He hadn't expected such speed.

George threw the next ball much more slowly. He curved it over the outside corner of the plate, away from the batter. The academy boy, expecting another fast pitch, swung too soon. He missed it by a mile.

"You're out!" called the umpire.

Slim threw the ball to Billy Pazdan at third. Billy snapped it over to Joey Jacobs at first. Then it went to Bobby Horn at short, and then to Bill Padget at second. Bill tossed it back to George.

"You're looking like a million, George!" they shouted.

The next academy boy hit a weak grounder to Joey Jacobs at first. An easy out. George struck out the third man, and it was St. Mary's turn to bat.

"Hurrah!" shouted all the members of the band.

"What do you think of that, mister?" Mario said to the man behind him and Rod.

"Not bad, not bad," was the reply. "But it's too early to tell!"

"Just you wait," Rod chimed in.

But the academy freshmen had a good pitcher, too. He was nearly as fast as George. Bobby Horn struck out as leadoff man. Terry Kelly, the center fielder, and Bill Padget hit easy flies for outs. The boys from St. Mary's were going to have to work for this victory.

In the top of the second inning, George struck out the side. Three men in a row fanned at his fast pitches.

"Everything's fine except my hand," Slim Morgan said as the boys trotted to the bench. "You're pitching hard today, George."

"I hope I can hit one now," said George, picking up his bat.

He got set at the plate. The first pitch was outside, for a ball. But it cracked loudly into the catcher's mitt. "Whew!" George thought. "He's plenty fast."

The next pitch looked pretty good. George took a full swing—and missed completely. He spun all the way around.

Shouts went up from the academy rooters. "Look at him swing!" said one fan. "He'll never hit it in a thousand years!"

George got set again. "I'll bet he throws me a curve this time," he thought. Sure enough, there it came, curving slowly toward the plate. George watched it carefully and swung again. But he hit it on top, and it bounced away for a foul.

"Now he'll try to throw it past me," George guessed. Sure enough the pitcher threw with all his speed. But George was ready. He swung again—as hard as he could.

Blam! The bat met the ball solidly. George dashed for first. He watched the ball soaring up—up—and it cleared the fence with plenty to spare. It was a home run!

Rod thumped his bass drum. Some of the boys in the band blew their horns. Others shouted. St. Mary's was ahead, 1–0.

Mario and Rod turned around to speak to the man behind them. The boys noticed that he didn't realize they were trying to get his

attention. He just kept staring at George.

George got up to bat again in the fourth. But the academy pitcher walked him.

The score stayed at 1-0, as inning after inning went by. George struck out man after man. Only one academy player even hit the ball.

Finally came the seventh—the last inning, because this game was shortened to let the university play. Bill Padget got a walk.

Brother Herman spoke to George. "We need another run," he said. "Let's see you sacrifice Bill down to second."

George nodded. He was aching to hit hard, but Brother Herman was right. At the plate George took a couple of practice swings—full swings. The academy fielders moved back.

There came the pitch. George jumped into bunting position. He just tapped the ball down the third-base line. He streaked for first—and made it safely.

But the next three boys went out in order. George went to the mound for the last half of the last inning, with only a one-run lead.

The academy rooters in the stands and the academy players on the bench shouted for a rally. They yelled at George, trying to get him rattled.

"Let 'em yell," George thought. "I'll just pitch that much better." He was having a wonderful time. He wound up and pitched. He struck out the first two men.

"That's eighteen strikeouts!" Mario shouted.

"Now, what do you think?" said Rod to the man behind them.

"By George, he's really pretty good!" the man said.

"'By George' is right," Mario said. "That's George Ruth!"

The next academy player hit a weak grounder to Bill Padget. Bill rushed for it, eager to throw the ball to first for the last out. In his eagerness he overran the ball—and the academy had a man on first. Their first base runner!

George was badly disappointed. That man

should have been out. The game should be over. He felt his temper start to flare up. But he stopped himself. "Well," he thought, "I guess I know better than to get angry now. I've got to pitch!"

Cheers went up from the stands. The academy's best hitter walked to the plate.

George studied him a minute. Then he threw a fast ball right across the plate. The academy batter hit at it—and connected. *Crack!* The ball flew on a line toward the farthest corner of left field.

George's heart sank as he turned to watch the flight of the ball. Soapy Soper in left field ran back and back as hard as he could go. He jumped up against the fence and reached high with his glove. *Smack!* The ball hit his glove, just as it was about to go over the fence for a home run. He held onto it!

"Hurrah!" shouted George, throwing his glove into the air. He rushed out to meet Soapy. "You saved my neck!" he cried and threw his arms around him.

"We win, 1–0!" Mario yelled.

The boys in the band rushed out onto the field. All the St. Mary's boys laughed and shouted and cheered.

"Nice game," said Brother Matthias to each of the players. He came to George. "That was real pitching, son. And a pretty good hit, too."

George grinned back at him. "I didn't let the boys down, did I, Brother?" he asked happily.

"No, son. You certainly didn't," Brother Matthias replied.

"Hey, George," shouted Rod. "How would you like to beat the bass drum?"

"Lead me to it!"

All through the next game George sat in the

stands in his baseball suit, happily beating the drum.

The man who had talked with Rod and Mario watched the second game carefully. But he kept looking at the tall, lanky George, too.

"H'm!" was all he said. But he wrote something down in his notebook.

THE BABE

ONE COLD FEBRUARY afternoon in 1914, George called to Rod, "How about catching for me?"

"Today?"

George grinned. "You can't start too early!"

On the windswept field George pitched ball after ball to Rod.

"All right, George, let's see that curve," Rod shouted.

George wound up. He curved the ball beautifully, just over the corner of the plate.

"That's the way!" said Rod, tossing the ball back. "Say, who's that coming?"

Brother Paul, Brother Herman, and Brother Matthias were walking across the field. A strange man was with them.

"Must be someone important they're showing around," George said. He threw a fast ball to Rod. It was a beautiful pitch, right over the heart of the plate.

The four men stopped near the baseball field. George kept on pitching.

"Are they watching us?" Rod asked.

Before George could answer, Brother Paul called to him, "Come on into the office with us, George."

"See you later, Rod," said George. "I wonder what's up!"

As he walked into the office, George thought, "Maybe they've got a tailoring job for me."

"Mr. Dunn," said Brother Paul to the stranger, "this is George Ruth. George, Mr. Dunn is the manager of the Baltimore Orioles baseball club."

"Baseball club," George thought. "What's this all about?"

"You were doing some pretty nice pitching out there," said Mr. Dunn.

Brother Matthias spoke up. "George, Mr.

Dunn would like to have you play on his team this season. Would you like to do that?"

"Why—why, I don't know. What kind of a team?"

Mr. Dunn looked surprised. "Why, ours is a professional-league team."

Brother Herman said, "You see, Mr. Dunn, the boys in the school seldom have time to read the newspapers."

George was getting excited now. "Which league?" he asked.

"Well, George," said Mr. Dunn, "we're in the International League. But of course all our players have a chance to go on up to the big leagues, if they're good enough."

"And you want me to play for you?" George asked. He could hardly believe what he was hearing. The professional leagues!

Mr. Dunn nodded.

"Why—why—I would love to play for you. Only—" He hesitated and looked at Brother Matthias.

"It will be a fine chance for you, if you want to do it, George," said Brother Matthias.

"Good!" Mr. Dunn said. "Then that's settled. Now, we'd better talk about his salary."

"Salary?" George burst out. "You mean you'll pay me for playing baseball?"

Mr. Dunn looked surprised again. "Why, of course," he said. "Let's see, I think we could pay you six hundred dollars for the season."

Six hundred dollars! George couldn't believe his ears.

"And of course if you make good, you can earn even more."

George's head was swimming.

Brother Paul nodded to Mr. Dunn. "That sounds satisfactory," he said.

"You know, I like very much to develop young players," Mr. Dunn said. "One of my scouts happened to see you pitch several years ago, George, and we've kept track of you since. You look good to me."

One of his scouts? That man at Emmitsburg—the one Rod had told him about! That's what he was—he was a scout for the Baltimore Orioles. And now the Orioles wanted George to play for them! It was just too good to be true. George thought he was dreaming.

"George, you be ready for spring training the end of this month," Mr. Dunn went on. "We're going to Fayetteville, North Carolina. I'll see you then." He shook George's hand and left.

"Well, George," asked Brother Matthias with a smile, "what do you think of it?"

"Gee!" spluttered George. "Why—I—why I don't—"

The three brothers laughed.

"It is a little sudden," said Brother Herman.

"It's wonderful!" George finally managed to say. "But I wonder how I'll get along with all those big stars?"

Brother Matthias put his arm around George's shoulders. "You'll make good," he said.

GEORGE GETS HIS NICKNAME

On the first day of March at Fayetteville, the Baltimore players were loosening up on the baseball diamond.

Jack Dunn walked onto the field. Behind him trotted George. He still looked very wide-eyed and surprised.

Two of the Baltimore players watched the gangling boy. One of them shook his head. "There comes Dunnie with another of his babes," he said as George walked away.

"Jack picks them young. What's this kid's name?" the second player asked.

"Why, I think it's Ruth. He's a pitcher, I understand." He paused. "Babe Ruth—how's that for a name?"

The other player laughed. "It fits him fine. Babe Ruth it is!"

FOR THE SAKE
OF THE KIDS

ON SEPTEMBER 9, 1918, Fenway Park in Boston was jammed with 22,000 spectators. They were watching the fourth game of the World's Series, between the Boston Red Sox and the Chicago Cubs.

It was the last of the fourth inning. The score was 0–0. There were two out. The Red Sox had two men on base—George Whiteman on second and Stuffy McInnis on first. Up to the plate strode a tall, broad-shouldered young player. It was Babe Ruth, Boston pitcher.

Mighty shouts arose from the Boston rooters.

"Win your own game, Babe!"

"Let's have a home run!"

"You can do it, Babe!"

George Tyler, the Cub pitcher, stood watching the batter. Finally he pitched.

"Ball one!" the umpire called.

"Ball two!"

"Ball three!"

Babe watched the fourth pitch carefully. He took a tremendous swing. He missed.

The next ball looked bad to the Babe. He let it go.

"Strike two!" the umpire called.

Babe frowned. He waggled his bat. He shifted his feet around. He waited for the next pitch.

Here it came! It was a straight fastball. Babe swung hard. *Crack!* The ball headed high and

far, straight for center field. Babe tore for first.

On and on the ball went, over the head of Max Flack, the Cubs' center fielder. But it didn't quite clear the fence. It hit the wall, and Babe ran around the bases as fast as he could go.

Whiteman and McInnis scored easily, and Babe pulled up at third.

"Can that Babe hit the ball!" shouted a sandy-haired man in a box seat. He tore up his score-card and threw the pieces over the field.

"Some wallop," said the short, fat man sitting next to him. "But Babe had better stick to his pitching."

"Pitching!" shouted the sandy-haired man. "Sure, he's a good pitcher! But everybody likes to see him wallop the ball."

Just then Everett Scott flied out, and the Red Sox took the field. They led, 2–0.

Through the fifth, the sixth, and the seventh, the score stayed the same. The Cubs couldn't score. When the last Cub was out in the seventh, the fat man jumped up and shouted, "It's a new record. It's a new record, Sandy!"

"What are you talking about?"

"Why, the Babe has just broken Christy Mathewson's World's Series record! Ruth has just pitched his twenty-ninth consecutive scoreless inning in World's Series play! I knew he could do it!"

Sandy whistled. "Boy, that's something!"

"And you want him to be a hitter! Why, he's the best young southpaw to come to the major leagues in years."

"Aw, I'd rather see him hit home runs."

"And he's pitching with a sore finger, too."

"Listen," said Sandy, "he hit eleven home runs this year—he tied for the highest in the league.

He hit more than Home Run Baker! Why—why, if he played every day, there's no telling how many he might hit. Maybe twenty-five—or even thirty!"

"You're crazy," said the fat man. "Who could ever hit that many?"

The Cubs finally broke through to score in the eighth inning. They made two runs and tied the game, 2–2. Babe was having trouble with his control. His finger was hurting more and more.

In the bottom of the eighth, the Red Sox pushed over another run to lead, 3–2.

In the top of the ninth, Babe walked Fred Merkle and Rollie Zieder, the first two men up. The Red Sox manager came in to talk to the Babe. He decided to put in a new pitcher. But instead of sending Babe to the bench, he put him in left field.

"Look at that!" shouted Sandy. "Did you ever

see that before? Ruth is going to stay in the game."

The fat man shook his head sadly. "That's the best way to ruin a pitcher," he said.

Joe Bush went to the mound for the Red Sox. He quickly got the side out. The Red Sox won, 3–2—and Babe Ruth had won his third World's Series game without a defeat.

"I just hope they let him keep on pitching," said the fat man. "He'll be a left-handed Christy Mathewson."

"And I hope you're wrong," shouted Sandy. "When he's up there batting, he really gives it everything he's got. Why, I'd even pay to see Babe Ruth strike out!"

TO HELP THE SCHOOL

It was September 27, 1920. The stands at Shibe Park in Philadelphia were clearing.

The New York Yankees had just beaten the Athletics, 3–0.

Sitting in a reserved section just behind home plate were the boys of the St. Mary's school band. They were playing away for all they were worth.

In front of the players' dugout on the field stood a tall husky figure in a Yankee baseball uniform. Toward him walked an even taller man in a long black robe. "Hello, George!" he said.

"Brother Matthias!" said the Yankee player. It was Babe Ruth.

"Maybe I should call you 'Babe'—since that's the name I see in all the papers."

"I'm so glad to see you that I don't care what you call me! How did you happen to come?"

"I came up to get the boys in the band. A̶ ̶ I want to thank you for arranging their the Yankees. They've collected a l will help greatly toward rebui

George spoke up. "That was terrible—the whole school's burning down. I wanted to help. And you know how I've always loved the band. So I thought it would be a good idea if they toured with the Yankees."

"It was a wonderful idea. And I want to thank you for the money you sent, too, George. It was very kind of you."

"Aw, gee, I'd do anything to help youngsters— and St. Mary's. I don't know where I'd have been without St. Mary's!"

"How do you like it on the Yankees, George? And how do you like playing outfield, instead of pitching?"

"They're treating me fine in New York, and we've got a great team," said the Babe enthusiastically. "I did hate to stop pitching, but you know how I love to hit."

"Well, George, you've certainly changed the

game of baseball, with your home runs. We were all very proud of you when you hit twenty-nine last year. We were very proud that a St. Mary's boy had broken all the old records. But this year it's unbelievable. Fifty-three already!"

"Maybe I can hit a few more, Brother Matthias. There are several games left."

Just then there was loud shouting from one of the exit gates. Pressed up against the gate was a crowd of youngsters. They were of all ages and sizes. "There he is!" they cried. "Hey, Babe, give us your autograph!"

George waved. "Hiya, kids! I'll be over in a few minutes. Just you wait."

Brother Matthias said, "It's wonderful how children love you, George. All the boys at St. Mary's look up to you. And I want to tell you how fine I think it is—the interest you've taken in visiting sick children. You're a real hero to them."

"Imagine me being a hero," said George, embarrassed. "But I do like to visit sick kids, and take them a bat or a ball or something, and talk about baseball."

"I'm sure you've helped a lot of them to get well," said Brother Matthias. He paused. He

cleared his throat. "That—er—that leads me to something I—er—wanted to say."

George looked at him in surprise. "Why, Brother Matthias, I've never known you to hesitate before." He stopped a minute. Then he went on slowly, "I wonder. Have the Yankee managers been talking to you?" George looked angry.

Brother Matthias smiled. "Yes, they have. And I hesitated, because, well, you're a man now. But maybe you wouldn't mind a word of advice from an old friend."

Now George smiled too. "Maybe I'm still too headstrong, Brother Matthias. I guess you're about the only one I'd really listen to. Go ahead!"

"Well, George, some people think maybe you have too many good times and don't take care of yourself the way you should. I see you've gained a lot of weight."

George frowned. "Yes, I've gained a lot—I weigh over two hundred now. But that helps me hit the ball harder. And you know how I love to eat!"

"George, nobody would grudge your having some good times. You have them coming to you. I know we were pretty strict at St. Mary's. Just don't overdo it—that's all. Don't let anything interfere with your keeping fit and playing your best game. You owe it to yourself and all the boys in America not to do that.

"You know, George, youngsters everywhere idolize you. You wouldn't ever want to let them down."

George thought a minute. "I guess I haven't thought too much about that," he said slowly. "But you're right, Brother Matthias. I wouldn't ever want to let the kids down."

Brother Matthias smiled and shook George's

hand. "I knew you'd understand, George. It's been wonderful to see you!"

"I'm glad you came, Brother Matthias. And I promise to do my best. I suppose I'll make some mistakes—but I won't forget your advice."

"That's fine, George. Now, you'd better go along and see the boys!"

George waved to Brother Matthias. He ran

over to the gate. "Hiya, kids!" he shouted, a big smile on his face.

The boys shoved forward, each wanting to be first. Babe wrote his name as fast as he could on scorecards, on pieces of paper, and in autograph books.

As fast as he could, he answered their questions. He was having the time of his life!

SIXTY HOME RUNS

It was September 30, 1927—the next to the last day of the baseball season. At Yankee Stadium in New York the Yankees were playing the Washington Senators.

Before the game the reporters in the press box were talking.

"Do you think he'll do it, Art?" asked a man wearing glasses. "Do you think the Babe will set a new home-run record today?"

"I don't know, Specs," said his neighbor. "But the way he's been hitting the ball lately, anything can happen."

"He already has fifty-nine this year," said Specs. "That ties his own record of 1921."

"The Yankees certainly don't need a home run today," said Art. "They've got the pennant sewed up already. They've won one hundred and eight games. And they're a cinch to win the World's Series."

"I call these Yanks the greatest team in history," said Specs. "Here they come!" The Yankees took the field for the first inning.

It was a close game. George Pipgras started pitching for New York. Tom Zachary pitched for Washington.

Every time Babe came to bat, the spectators shouted themselves hoarse. "Hit another one, Babe! We want a home run!"

But the Babe hit two singles, to help the Yankees score two runs.

Manager Miller Huggins of the Yankees sent Herb Pennock in to pitch. He was trying out all his pitchers—to get them ready for the World's Series.

The Washington Senators tied up the score, 2–2. There it stood when the Yankees came to bat in the bottom of the eighth.

Earl Combs led off for the Yankees. He flied out to center field.

Then Mark Koenig came up. He picked out one of Tom Zachary's fastballs and slammed it to left center, all the way to the wall. He got a triple.

Then up to the plate walked Babe Ruth. Miller Huggins, the manager, had given him the sign to hit away.

"If I get a long fly," thought the Babe, "it will

bring in Mark for the leading run. But I hope I can put one out of the park!"

He took a couple of practice swings. The noise from the fans was deafening. Babe just grinned. "I'll give them something to yell about."

Zachary pitched, putting all his strength behind the ball. Babe swung with all his might.

Crack! The bat met the ball solidly. Up and up it soared, into the second deck of the stands. It was a tremendous home run.

The reporters jumped up and shouted.

"Look at that!" shouted Specs. "Number sixty! It's a new record. Oh, that Babe!"

"What a man!" Art shouted.

The spectators were cheering and waving and throwing their hats in the air.

The Babe trotted briskly around the bases. As he came down the third-base line he took off his cap. There was a wide smile on his round face.

Cheers went up even louder. The Babe tipped his cap time after time, and the spectators cheered louder and louder for the Babe.

He crossed home plate and headed for the dugout. The Yankee team was waiting in a double line to congratulate him.

There were Earl Combs and Mark Koenig. There was Lou Gehrig, the Yankee first baseman.

"I've got to thank you, Lou," said Babe. "If you hadn't pushed me so hard with your home runs, maybe I'd never have set a new record. And you're a wonderful friend."

There was Bob Meusel to greet the Babe. And Tony Lazzeri and Jumping Joe Dugan and Benny Bengough and George Pipgras and Herb Pennock. And little Miller Huggins, the manager.

They slapped Babe on the back. "Nice going, Babe!" they all shouted.

Up in the press box the sportswriters finally sat down. They were weak from shouting.

"You know," Specs said, "I'm going to vote for the Babe for Player of the Year, when the New York Baseball Writers have their dinner this winter."

"Brilliant! Brilliant!" said Art jokingly. "Why, of course we'll vote him Player of the Year. Who else!"

Specs held up his hand. "Not just because he hit sixty home runs this year. Not just because he has batted .356. Do you know why?"

"Well—" said Art.

"I'll tell you—it's because of his comeback. Why, after the 1925 season everybody thought the Babe was through. He had hit only twenty-five home runs and batted only .290. He wasn't taking care of himself and was so sick he could hardly play," Specs said.

Art grinned. "He had 'the stomachache that was heard around the world,'" he said. "At least, that's the way we wrote about it in the papers."

"You know the saying as well as I do," Specs went on, "that 'champions never come back.' Well, Babe Ruth did! He took off all the extra weight. He got himself in good condition again. And now look! A new home-run record!"

"Yes," said Art, "that's about the toughest thing a man can do. You've got to hand it to him. He's a real man."

"And I'll bet he did it for the kids as much as for any other reason," said Specs. "The kids love him—and he'd do anything for them. Boy, how they'll love him now!"

MR. BASEBALL

TWENTY YEARS LATER Yankee Stadium
was jammed with the biggest crowd of the season. There were nearly 60,000 people. They
had all come out for Babe Ruth Day—April
27, 1947.

It was Babe Ruth Day all over the world—
wherever baseball was played. Every ballpark
in the United States observed it. Many Latin-
American countries celebrated the day. And
in Japan the Professional Baseball League had

named it "Babu Rusu Day." The Japanese had never forgotten the Babe's visit in 1934.

In the New York stands the spectators were chattering while they waited for the ceremony to begin. Some of the fans had met Babe Ruth personally. Others had seen him play or read about him in the papers. But they all had one thing in common—they were eager to see the Babe on the playing field again.

"Isn't it great that the Babe is coming back to baseball?" said a young man to his neighbor in the stands. "He stopped playing in 1935. I'll never forget the time he came to see me, when I was sick."

"Did he really?"

"Indeed he did! I didn't think I'd ever get well. But after he came to the hospital, I couldn't wait to get out and play baseball again."

"I guess nobody will ever know how many

children he helped. What's he doing now, do you know?"

"Why, haven't you heard?" the young man said. "He's going to help American Legion Junior Baseball. The Ford Motor Company has hired him to go around the country. He'll give talks and teach the kids how to play."

"Why, that's wonderful," said the neighbor. "Will he be well enough to do it?"

"I certainly hope so. He's been pretty sick, after that throat operation. But he'll do it if he can. He'll never let the kids down."

His neighbor thought a minute. "You know, I read that the Babe got 30,000 letters in the hospital, mostly from children," he said. "Imagine that, when he hasn't played baseball for twelve years."

"There's something special about the Babe," said the young man. "He's Mr. Baseball himself.

I guess everybody loves him because he always did everything in such an exciting way."

"Right! Why, they say the Yankees were able to build this stadium back in 1923 because so many people came to see the Babe. The sportswriters even call it 'the house that Ruth built.'"

Down on the field the ceremony was about to start. A microphone was set up at home plate. The Yankee players lined up on one side of the plate. Their opponents, the Washington Senators, were on the other side.

Francis Cardinal Spellman spoke a prayer for America, for baseball, and for Babe Ruth. He asked a blessing on the nation "as we honor a hero in the world of sport, a champion of fair play, and a manly leader of youth in America."

From the Yankee dugout Babe Ruth walked to home plate. A tremendous cheer went up from the crowd. The Babe took off his cap and bowed to them, just as he used to when he hit a home run. The old, broad grin lighted his big round face.

The commissioner of baseball said a few words. So did Ford Frick, president of the National League, and Will Harridge, president of the American League.

Then a lad spoke up for American Legion Junior Baseball. "To know that Babe Ruth is going to be with us kids—well, that's the biggest and best thing that could happen in baseball."

Then the Babe stepped to the microphone. He talked to the crowd. "The only real game in the world is baseball. And you've got to start young. If you try hard enough you're bound to come out on top, just as these boys here have come to the top now." He pointed toward the

two teams. "And now, for all the lovely things said about me today, I thank everybody."

The Babe nodded to the crowd and started for the dugout. Cheer upon cheer rang out from the spectators. It was all the Babe could do to keep the tears out of his eyes. "Sometimes I forgot the advice Brother Matthias gave me," he thought, "but I hope I made up for my mistakes."

The Yankees crowded around him. They all wanted to shake his hand—Phil Rizzuto, King Kong Keller, Tommy Henrich, Yogi Berra, and all the others.

Joe DiMaggio asked for his autograph. So did Frankie Crosetti and Bucky Harris, the Yankee manager.

Up in the press box the reporters were cheering as loudly as the rest of the fans.

"Remember that day twenty years ago when the Babe hit his sixtieth home run?" said Specs.

"Well, I just had to come back today for this celebration."

"So did I," said Art. "But I don't know how to write my story today. There's so much to tell about the Babe. He's made so many records. I hardly know where to begin!"

"You could write a book of nothing but records," said Specs. "Why, he holds or shares sixty-one baseball records right now. And he's been retired for years."

"It'll be a long time before anyone beats his record of sixty home runs in one season," said Art. "Or the total of seven hundred and fourteen home runs of his career."

"He got more bases on balls than anyone. He batted in more runs than anyone. He even struck out more times than anyone."

"Everything he did, he did in a big way. That's why people flocked to see him."

"That's right," Specs agreed. "He didn't hit just ordinary home runs. His were tremendous! All the experts say he hit the ball harder than any other player who ever lived."

"I remember one home run he hit in Florida," said Art. "That was back in 1919, when the Babe was still with the Red Sox. We measured the distance the ball traveled. It was nearly six hundred feet. Someone will really have to hustle to beat that record."

Another reporter spoke up. "He hit more than home runs, too! What about his batting average? He hit .342 for his twenty-two years in the leagues. Not many have ever topped that!"

"And he played in *ten* World's Series!" said still another. "He helped the Yankees win their very first league championship—and six more!"

"Enough! Enough!" Specs protested. "This could go on forever. The Babe's name is in the record books so many times that no one could ever forget him."

"It was in 1936 that he was elected to the National Baseball Hall of Fame, wasn't it?" Art added. "That's the greatest honor a baseball player could ever receive."

"He's admired by everyone," spoke up another reporter who had just come in. "He's a sort of symbol of determination, courage, and good sportsmanship all rolled in one."

"Say," said Art, "we'd better go if we're going to talk to the big fellow before the game starts. We don't have much time."

They hurried to where the Babe was sitting.

"Babe," said Specs, "I've heard a rumor about your starting a Babe Ruth Foundation. Can you tell us something about it?"

"Well, boys," said the Babe, "it's not to be announced for a few days yet. But I can tell you it's going to be started."

"What's it for?"

"I can only say that it will be set up to benefit poor boys. I was one myself. It will sponsor sport—and scholarship, too."

"That's great," said Art. "Where's the money coming from?"

Babe grinned. "You might not believe it," he said, "but I managed to save a little through the years. I'm starting off the foundation with a gift. And I'm sure baseball teams will chip in with benefit games."

"Of course they will," agreed Specs. "Tell me, Babe—what do you think of your new job—working with the American Legion Junior Baseball program?"

The Babe flashed his famous smile. "I'm

going to love working with those kids," he said. "It's the kind of job I've always wanted!"

The boys of American Legion Junior Baseball enjoyed the teachings of the Babe for only a short time. Then he had to give up the job he loved so much. Just a little over a year later, on August 16, 1948, Babe Ruth died.

ABOUT THE AUTHOR

GUERNSEY VAN RIPER JR. attended DePauw University in 1926. He earned two varsity letters as a quarterback on the football team and one letter as a first baseman on the baseball team. After graduating, he worked in advertising then became an editor at the Bobbs-Merrill Publishing Company. He turned his love of sports into books, writing biographies of Lou Gehrig and Knute Rockne along with ten other children's books.